OKTOBERFEST

Frank De Felitta

OKTOBERFEST

1973
Doubleday & Company, Inc., Garden City, New York

The characters in this novel are fictional, including all characters who function in official capacities, such as: officials of the city of Munich and its police department, and all officials mentioned in both the *Tombeau du Martyr Juif Inconnu*, in Paris, and Yad Vashem in Israel. Any resemblance to actual persons living or dead is purely coincidental.

ISBN: 0-385-07060-8
Library of Congress Catalog Card Number 73–80012
Copyright © 1973 by Frank De Felitta
All Rights Reserved
Printed in the United States of America
First Edition

For My Wife

ACKNOWLEDGMENTS

I wish to express my gratitude to Mr. Steven Weiner, Professor Irwin R. Blacker, Mr. and Mrs. Ben Schanzer, Mr. Gene Lesser, Mr. Tim Seldes, and my editor, Miss Diane Cleaver, for their confidence, encouragement, and assistance in the writing of this book.

Accursed race, up to your tricks again!
How often have we proved, beyond disputing,
No ghost can stand upon a normal footing?
And yet you dare to dance like mortal men!

—GOETHE (Faust / Walpurgis Night)

MUNICH:
The First Day of Oktoberfest

CHAPTER ONE

In the autumn of the year, the skies of Bavaria turn a deep blue
and the trees over the roads red and gold. A mist crowds the
Alpine slopes. A cold wind comes up through the green and
rolling hills, the yellow fields of hay, and across the little white,
shining, compact towns. In Munich the copper towers gleam in
the sun. It is the time for Oktoberfest. Down among the
Renaissance façades and rococo turrets six million persons crowd
the streets, buying, drinking, and dancing. For sixteen days the
people lose themselves in the processions, alcohol, and noise of
celebration, until they lie bleary and exhausted, the foreigners
begin to leave, and little white flakes begin to fall high in the
mountains. Then the Münchners pick themselves up, clean the
streets, and return to their Bohemian cafes in the Schwabing or
the aluminum insurance offices along Maxburgerstrasse, and patiently await the Christmas holidays.

When Ludwig of Bavaria married Therese von Saxe-Hildburghausen, the peasants and townspeople celebrated with a horse race and a picnic. It was a great success. Every year after, there was an October feast. Should Ludwig now roam in spirit over Therese's Meadow, at the end of the celebration, under the Ferris wheels and among the beer pavilions, into the tents where men and women lie sleeping drunk, unable to remember where they live, he might know that the Bavarians have not changed so much in 150 years. Should he wander off the fairgrounds, however, and see where chrome buildings inexplicably arise where once were the fountains and courtyards that he built, he would know that after 150 Oktoberfests Munich had changed. In fact, all of Germany had been altered.

* * *

The morning mist rose onto the mountain slopes and gathered in the valleys. They say that the mountains themselves exhale this vapory air, and the sunlight, shafting through in long rays, falls on forests and streams that were present at the creation itself. Deep from her pine bower the Virgin Mary, rough-cut and whittled, painted red and blue, looks disinterestedly on the country scene below. Red and green farm equipment chugs busily over the fertile fields. Modern homes, with sheet-metal sidings, dominate the hills. And rounding through the woods, its great iron gates rusted but serviceable, the gray walls of Brautnacht Sanitarium look out over the surrounding valleys.

The man sat in a wrought-iron garden chair. His deep, dark eyes faced the brilliant autumn mist. He was as he had been positioned by the nurse. The sun had altered, but the man's head had not moved. The hands, huge and powerful, hung down at his sides. An open album of faded photographs lay motionless across his lap. All around sang the beautiful birds in the trees.

Nearby on the lawn a boy lay, wriggling. His hands were strapped into a leather sling, so that they could not reach his mouth. Desperately, he wanted to eat them. Struggling to free himself, he rolled into the dirt beneath the rose bushes.

Out from a cement hall a nurse came quickly, her face pale, with her lips, though closed, working rapidly. She bent down and jerked the boy off the ground and squeezed him at the clavicle. Slowly the frenzied mouth opened, and she slapped the dirt out of it. Only when she let him go did the babbling cease. He sank again to the level of the rose bushes. She watched him a long, stern moment before departing. Smiling, tears in his eyes, the boy wormed his way quickly over the lawn, his arms out in front of him, and stopped finally to explore the white fungus in spots at the base of a tree.

No sound had penetrated the man in the wrought-iron chair. However, a blue vein in his finger twitched rapidly. Birds occasionally flew or hopped across the lawn, and his eyes, wide and vacant, recorded their comings and goings like a camera without film.

Then a bird hopped up to his slipper, pecked at the leather, extravagantly extracted from the fluff a long, clean strand, and then, in the shadow of the man's foot, looked alertly around, up and down, before bouncing back out into the sunlight. Suddenly a gray streak came over the lawn and a paw slapped. The cat lifted up its paw and scrupulously studied the stunned bird underneath. Blood began to show on the feathers and on the paws. The bird began to scream. The cat looked about, picked up the bird in its mouth, and quickly carried it under the man's chair.

The man's hand trembled. The screaming of the bird was not stopped, though surely it was being eaten. Beads of perspiration broke out on the man's forehead. The vein in his temple began to throb in rhythm to the dying sounds beneath the chair. Suddenly his hand clutched at the album in a spastic motion, and he rose in his chair, ripping from the falling album a single photograph. The bird screams rose, and then stopped abruptly.

3

The man remained standing, trembling over the ground, veins fairly bulging, eyes still wide and staring, but now alert and filled with animal fear. Slowly, raising the photograph up to his vision, he stared at it until it was a blur before him, and it crumpled in his hand.

The nurse poked her face out from the window in the cement hallway. Squinting through her glasses, she worked her lips in alarm, then stopped. The wrought-iron chair stood empty, silhouetted against the brightness of the sky. The man was gone. Cautiously, she emerged.

The boy in leather strapping lolled at the end of the grounds. There was no one else about. Only the birds and an occasional breeze disturbed the rolling green. She looked around, her eyes ferreting the distant, darker fringes of the compound. She backed into the main building once again.

Behind her the nervous face of Dr. Gunther Kaufmann, director of Brautnacht Sanitarium, emerged in the hallway, gazing quickly about over her shoulder.

"He's gone," she whispered.

"What happened?"

"I don't know. He can't have gotten far. I'll go look for him."

"Yes, go look for him," Dr. Kaufmann ordered.

Searching in vain for a white handkerchief to wipe his brow, Dr. Kaufmann leaned heavily against the rough wall and began to consider quickly certain legal complications.

*　　*　　*

Black-hatted, black-coated bands wound their way through the old quarter, across town to Therese's Meadow. Wagons of beer, pulled by white horses in blue and silver fringe, rolled up through the fairgrounds. Old women in black dirndl dresses pelted the drivers with flowers. Under the theaters and magic shows, families of Japanese, Americans, and Yugoslav laborers wandered, taking photographs. Huge balloons with beer labels floated over the crowd. Crossbowmen, between draughts of beer, aimed for the wavering cardboard stag at the end of the midway. Bosomy women ran among the tables of the beer pavilions, sweating, trying to serve the insistent clamor of banging steins and shouting Germans. Bands replaced exhausted bands, and soon the crowds, no longer strangers, stood on benches and tables, linked arm in arm and roaring out German drinking songs.

Out of the glistening air, lumbering their way across the old country roads, two powerful dray horses pulled behind them a wagon of empty beer barrels and five drunken Germans. The horses clopped slowly up the rise, away from the queer modern houses that stuck over the hills like weird plants in the sun, away from the gardens and the carnival raging full tilt across Therese's Meadow.

The driver wore a costume of indecipherable origin, of silks and brass buttons, and a nose painted red, the paint of which had drained on both sides down to his mouth. Across his tunic, badges, signifying the number of liters of double-strength brew he had consumed, tinkled merrily with each jerk and pull of the wagon.

In the back of the cart, leaning against the barrels, on boards and flowers, a man in Bavarian black lay across the laps of two women. Another man held onto the sides of the bouncing cart. With each bounce, someone's arm flopped across another body. Gradually the man, blinking his vision clearer, raised himself and shook the hair from his forehead.

"Good God." He laughed. "Look at that fool run. He must be in training."

Across the field of hay, tall grass waving at the brook, a large man in blue slacks and shirt raced across the road, running barefoot, head lowered, toward the woods on a hill that lay in the northern suburbs of Munich.

The forest, as he penetrated its density, seemed familiar to

5

him, but it was not friendly. It slapped at his face, ripped his clothing, and bruised the skin of his hands. At length, panting, he stopped. At the edge of the forest, the city appeared. It spread down from the hills, brown, and joined in the center where the green peaked roofs were jagged together like teeth, and the Christian façades glittered elegantly in the light. Fearful, bewildered, the man began to move cautiously down through culverts, biding his time, dashing across railroads and over bridges, and gradually making his way unseen into the suburbs of Munich.

* * *

They were fighting over food. Two boys were punching each other furiously, blood coming out of a chipped tooth. They were locked together, and as one freed himself, he swung with his full weight on the other.

"Karl! Karl!" A woman leaned out of an upstairs apartment window. Her bosom suspended over the cement sill. "Stop it! You leave him go!" She disappeared.

A boy, free, slapped the other hard on the head, and they both went down on the ground.

"Karl! You get up!" The woman came, running, across the rubble of the new construction site. She pulled the two apart. "Leave him go!" she yelled.

"He stole from me," the other boy cried.

"Stole! My boy's no thief! You stole! You Prussian!" She took her son's arm and pulled him away. "Go home," she shouted at the other boy. "Go away from here!"

"He stole," the boy cried again. "Two apples and a pear. They're gone."

The woman pushed by him. "You lost them. You stupid!" She walked with her son across the rutted ground back toward the apartment buildings. "Never trust these people," she instructed him.

6

Through a square of ventilation the man watched all this. With neither amusement nor excitement he peered out through a break in the wall of a gutted basement. The fight had occurred in his field of vision, so it had been recorded. He slumped down against a wall.

It was a shelter made of falling bricks, of beams having fallen diagonally and supporting now a crude overhead of broken stone and cable reinforcement. Debris lay all about—bricks, bits of wiring and lath, scraps of wallpaper. The man slowly stretched out his leg, trying not to disturb the precarious ceiling over his head. Dust sifted down over his shoulders.

From the square of ventilation, there was no place in the yard that could not be seen. But there was no quick exit, only the slow extrication from the square over his head. That was a danger. He would wait until night. Then it would be dark everywhere. No one would see him. He could move. Somewhere a dripping water pipe echoed among the ruins.

The man shivered. He bit into the pear. He ravenously gulped it down, and began on the two apples in his other hand.

* * *

A cathedral tower tolled the quarter hour before eight. Sounds of roistering boomed forth from the pavilions and fun houses of Therese's Meadow; however, in the old part of town it was quiet. The darkness of the old market was scarcely dispelled by the far street lamps of modern Munich. An old woman walked quickly across the cobbled roads. A cat sat on a wooden step, unmoving, watching. The square, hemmed in by massive stone walls and shadows growing out of alleys, was deserted.

In a small butcher shop Wolfgang Heder pounded steaks with the flat of his cleaver. Heder was a huge man, rosy-cheeked, and he kept his triple chin cleanly shaved. It was seven minutes to closing, and he worked methodically, setting steaks onto doilies and garnishing them with minted greens. Heder pursed his

7

small red lips in a humorless smile. It was an expensive shop, for only the wealthiest of patrons.

Street lamps shone feebly through the shop windows. Heder walked into the stainless steel, brightly illuminated refrigerator, and the automatic door quietly closed. Heder hefted slabs of beef onto tenterhooks and wiped the sides with his apron. Dimly he heard the bell of the door ring, signifying that someone had entered. He frowned, sorry now he had not locked the front door. A customer at this late hour would delay his arrival at the pavilion by at least fifteen minutes, and would give Olga, his wife, a legitimate excuse to be irritable. Muttering softly, Heder counted the boxes of greens set on the lower shelves. Then he pushed in the lock of the door from the inside and pushed it open.

Heder froze. High over his head, glinting in the light, was his own cleaver, held in two hands that whitened around the handle. Before he moved, the hands drove the cleaver down. It broke through him, ear and jaw, and red blood poured out quickly through broken bits of bone. Heder, his eyes dilating rapidly, fell backward onto the wooden slats of the refrigerator. The cleaver rose again and fell, and when it was through, Heder lay sightless in his own blood, and in his mouth was stuffed a dark and crumpled photograph.

*   *   *

All the shops were closed. A lone harlequin walked through the old market place on his way home. The blue and green lights of the police cars revolved in front of Heder's butcher shop. A uniformed policeman kept out a number of onlookers. Inside, the body of Heder was carefully, gingerly examined. A police photographer braced his feet in front of the refrigerator door and took pictures with a flash gun. All metallic, glass, and wooden surfaces were searched for fingerprints. In a corner of the shop Inspector Paul Steinman held a glass of mineral water for an elderly woman sitting in a chair.

"What made you go into the refrigerator?" Steinman asked.

"I don't know."

"It is not a normal thing to do."

"I don't know what made me go in there." The woman began to cry. "I didn't see him anywhere in the shop."

". . . So you went to look for him in the refrigerator?"

"Pray God I hadn't!"

The old woman crossed herself with a trembling hand.

At the refrigerator, police doctor Karl-Heinz Fischer emerged and requested a litter. Sweating, he stood in the doorway and wiped his forehead with a white handkerchief. He shook his head at Steinman with a pale look. The ambulance driver and attendant brought in the wicker litter, and Fischer once again stepped inside the refrigerator.

Chief Inspector Martin Bauer stood at the counter, studying the photograph without touching it. A lean man, his hairline just beginning to recede, his roughly hammered features were drawn into a puzzled expression. There seemed to be something in the crumpled, soggy photograph withdrawn from the victim's mouth that he knew, yet could not quite figure out.

Steinman tugged gently on the old woman's coat.

"Frau Knoedler, please answer me," he said. "Do you often shop here?"

"Yes. Tonight I was late. He usually closes at eight o'clock."

"I see. And you got here after eight?"

"Yes."

"Frau Knoedler, do you live near here? No? Then you will be escorted home." Steinman gestured to a uniformed policeman. "However, we may want to talk to you again in the morning. Thank you. You have done your civic duty."

Steinman closed his notebook and walked to his superior at the counter. Martin Bauer's eyes watched his approach unsee-

9

ing, his mind still playing on the fringes of recollection. Steinman coughed.

"Well, I believe we're through," he said.

"Excuse me?" Bauer snapped out of his thoughts. He smiled. "Was she guilty or innocent?"

"I haven't the vaguest idea. You know, with the prices he charged, I wouldn't blame her if she had."

Bauer laughed. He returned to the photograph. Forgetting Steinman, he pursed his lips as he looked it over carefully.

"Has Fischer finished the examination?"

Bauer, distracted again, said, "I don't think so."

Steinman looked over the counter at the photograph.

"Is that it?" Steinman said.

"Yes."

"See anyone you know?" Steinman grinned.

Bauer looked up.

"Now that's the funny thing, Paul. I have a strange feeling that I do. Take a look."

"It's been dusted?"

"Yes. It had prints."

Steinman leaned over and studied the photograph. It was a train station. A group of men and women waited in line. It was cold, for they wore coats and gloves. There was no snow on the ground. There were no signs visible. Apparently the photograph was old, judging by the style of the clothes and by the faded appearance of the black and white.

"So?" Steinman asked.

"It says nothing to you?"

"No." Steinman picked lint off the collar of his coat. "It wasn't taken yesterday. People at a station—what does it mean to you?"

Bauer shook his head.

Dr. Fischer stepped out of the refrigerator. Still perspiring heavily, he walked stiffly over to Steinman and Bauer at the counter.

"Imagine, sweating in a refrigerator. I haven't seen anything like this since medical school. Do you mind if we go out for a breath of fresh air?" They began walking toward the open door. "Whoever had it in for him did a good job—chopped him half to pieces—probably an ax—then hoisted him onto a hook like a side of beef."

"A cleaver is missing," Steinman said.

Fischer rubbed the back of his neck. They looked out in the cold night air as the crowd, still red-cheeked and costumed, looked almost eagerly back at them. "Well, that's what did it then. You think it was the work of one man?"

"Do you have an opinion?" Steinman asked.

Fischer had regained his composure in the cold autumnal air. "He had to have a lot of strength. Heder weighed well over a hundred kilograms." Fischer turned to Bauer. "I'll do my report and see you in the morning, Inspector."

"You'll see Steinman in the morning," Bauer said. "I'm leaving for Kitzbühel tonight."

"Kitzbühel?" Fischer said. "I didn't know you were an Alpinist."

"I'm not."

"It's too early for skiing."

"I know."

Steinman laughed. "There are other . . . pursuits in Kitzbühel. Not so, Martin?"

Bauer reddened and said nothing. Elements of the crowd were already melting back into the brighter quarters of Munich. Others had sobered as they understood what had happened. The ambulance doors were opened.

"Well," Fischer said, "I'd say your timing was perfect. Oktoberfest, and a grisly murder. A good time to go to Kitzbühel."

Behind them, in the shop, the ambulance attendant poked his head out of the refrigerator door. "Hey there, you!" he called.

"Could you spare me a man to give us a hand? We've got a regular Hermann Goering here!"

Bauer's eyes quickly narrowed. He tried once more to grasp hold of the idea that suddenly pricked at his memory again, barely out of reach. Again Steinman's voice shattered the moment.

"Koenig," he called. "Give them a hand. I'll be back in an hour." Steinman put a hand on Bauer's shoulder. "Come, get your things and I'll drive you to the station."

"Thank you."

"You are thinking of something," Steinman said. "What is it this time, Kitzbühel or the photograph?" Before Bauer could answer, Steinman turned to the red-faced Koenig, lifting up his end of the sagging wicker litter containing Heder's body. "Koenig, bring the photograph to headquarters. It is important to Inspector Bauer."

"Yes, sir," Koenig replied.

Koenig and the ambulance driver and attendant slowly carried the mountainous corpse through the room and out into the street. Steinman and Bauer looked down on the body.

"Throw a cloth over his face," Steinman said.

Koenig cleared the crowd, the huge body was settled inside the ambulance, and the doors were closed. The ambulance forced its way through the people and down the cobbled square, and turned onto a wide and bright avenue. The revelers drifted away. Fischer drove away toward home. Steinman grinned.

"If we hurry, we'll have time for a glass of beer before your train leaves," he said.

"If I hurry, I'll just have time to pack," Bauer replied.

*   *   *

The blue and white police car squealed to a stop in front of the block of flats overlooking the dark Isar.

"I'll come up and help you," Steinman said.

"Come." Bauer opened the car door and climbed out.

"Or shall I wait?"

"Wait."

"I'll come."

The half-packed suitcase lay open across the neatly made bed.

"Hand me that, will you?" Bauer said, pointing to a beautifully chased silver cigarette lighter at Steinman's elbow.

Steinman held it in his hand a moment before he gave it to Bauer.

"The crest of Bismarck," Steinman said, impressed.

"I won it in school. Many years ago." Bauer threw it down into the suitcase full of his sweaters and trousers, all of the finest quality. "Marksmanship."

"Yes," Steinman said. "You light a girl's cigarette with that and she knows you are something special."

The night lights from outside seemed to revolve in the room, and then Bauer realized that a passing automobile in the street below was turning a corner. For some reason, it disoriented him. Then the darkness came back again, and it seemed to comfort him.

"What's wrong, Martin?"

"Nothing. Where are my socks?"

Bauer went into his bedroom. There he pulled open the dark wood drawer of his chest and rummaged through it. Steinman watched him from the living room. Bauer seemed unusually lean, and tired, a silhouette in the far room.

"Something's bothering you, Martin," Steinman said. "The murder?"

Bauer smiled as he came back into the living room.

"Not enough beer," he said.

"Well, now I believe you."

Bauer glanced at the ticket in his breast pocket. Steinman followed him to the door, carrying the suitcase. Bauer took a brief look at his little flat and turned off the light. For an instant everything was a void, but then his eyes readjusted to the darkness and the metal and glass fixtures of the rooms, like so many identical rooms all over Germany, winked back at him, neat, functional, sterile. In every way, the flat reflected the essence of his life, Bauer thought; the sum and substance of his forty-seven years on earth. He shut the door behind him and locked it in two places.

Clown faces appeared rapidly in the brightness of their headlights and then disappeared just as rapidly. The car had to swerve to miss hitting them. A carnival for the stomach, Bauer thought with disgust—a two-week assault on the brains and the intestines, unfathomable—

The car swerved again, nearly skidding.

"Excuse me, sir," Steinman said, glancing over at him from the driver's seat.

"Why? What's wrong?"

"I nearly ran over that musician."

"I hadn't noticed."

Bauer looked back. A fat man, in a black waistcoat and black hat, held his tuba defensively in his arms. He shook a fist at the speeding car and shouted curses after them.

"That will sharpen up his flats," Bauer laughed.

Steinman chuckled. The scenery flashed past them. The old houses, the ruined walls, repainted, threw shadows, dark as death, into the alleys. Bauer, never married, thought of the days of his youth, when every such street had beckoned him on like a woman's distant song, strangely stirring his male fancy. . . .

The car sped into the boisterous crowds. Green and flesh-colored faces hove briefly in the night lights of the central city. Loathesome, they were to Bauer. Or was it something of himself he saw on them which was loathesome? Bauer began to look forward to the Alpine retreat as though to a religious retreat. Somehow, he felt the need of a purification. People crowded the squares, ran out from the Opera House, and revelers laughed and sang on the steps of the great stone buildings.

The crowds everywhere increased; the buttons and sequins and embroideries glittered from their costumes. Steinman screeched to a halt behind the railroad station. There, Bauer had the uncomfortable feeling that he was drowning in the ocean of faces. Then he stirred himself and got out of the car. Someone threw a bottle through the riotous noise, and the glass shivered up over a distant wall and sparkled in the night air. Steinman nudged Bauer and grinned.

"It's a good night!" Steinman said.

CHAPTER TWO

The noise was appalling. All the tracks of the Munich train station were disgorging visitors. Businessmen and students, laborers, nuns, and foreign tourists poured through the enormous glass doorways, formed lines at the information and currency windows, and milled, formless, into the bars and out to the waiting taxi lines, into the brilliantly lighted streets of Munich.

Pushing their way against the stream, Bauer and Steinman moved sluggishly past elbows and baggage wagons, Austrians and Swiss, toward the first platform of the second track. There they waited patiently. In front of them were groups of elderly hikers, with knapsacks and walking sticks, also patiently waiting. Speech was impossible in the uproar. Bauer felt a heady excitement, as the thousands of individuals even here had mingled into a single festive mass. Steinman clapped him on the shoulder. Overhead the white signs clacked into place. Around the bend, slowly, came the electric to Austria, gliding under the huge glass canopy.

The train stopped in front of them. Steinman opened the door and hefted in Bauer's suitcase. They made their way down the corridor to the first lighted compartment and opened the door. Inside a pretty, young girl, dark haired, sat on the bench, reading a magazine. Bauer nodded as he put down his suitcase, and stepped back into the corridor.

"Not bad, Martin," Steinman whispered.

"Not bad at all."

"You know what they say. During the Oktoberfest, there's not a girl who doesn't—"

"Yes, I know."

"Well, enjoy yourself." Steinman shook his hand, grinned, and winked. With a wave of the hand, he walked down the corridor and stepped off into the flickering densities of the crowd. Bauer stepped inside the compartment and closed the door. The girl looked up with a cool disdain in her eyes.

Bauer sat down at the window, across from the girl, and carefully smoothed the crease of his black trousers. He looked out the window, and for the first time felt separated and secure from the milling crowds that pressed together along the station platform. Bauer sighed with something close to contentment, and turned to study the girl.

She was dark, kittenish, with rosy cheeks and a pert, turned-up nose. She was quite sure of herself, her long, black-stockinged legs folded, one over the other. She wore an open tweed coat with a thin white sweater underneath. Her slender figure idly stroked the bench. She came from Bavarian stock, a lovely mixture of the races. Bauer took out his silver cigarette case.

"Fräulein?" he offered.

She made no sign of having heard him. Bauer picked a cigarette, returned the case, and looked uncomfortably around the room. It was an old car, dating back to the war years, with a wooden suitcase rack instead of aluminum, a heater that was not working, and the old-fashioned green plastic cushions. The train gave a lurch and began to slide out of the station. Bauer settled back and watched out the window.

The dark brick squares of buildings went by, and Bauer could see, across the shopping centers, the brilliant acres of fairgrounds at the edge of town. Several churches went by, a dark part of town, and then the train began to slow. The train stopped, in a maze of sidings and bridges. Bauer closed his eyes. He tried to think of the autumn leaves, the slopes, and the lakes near Kitzbühel.

A noise woke him. They were still at the sidings. Bauer looked at his watch. He stood stiffly to gaze out the window. Some sort of activity was increasing across the yard. Bauer wiped the glass clean and peered out into the darkness.

Freight cars, under floodlights mounted on telephone poles, opened their doors. Cattle confusedly stepped out onto the platform and then hustled down the ramps. Men grouped them with electric prods. Bellows lifted protestingly into the air and carried to where Bauer watched from the train window. Bauer's eyes narrowed. The cattle were pushed down the ramps, one stepping on the next, into barbed wire and wooden-slatted gangways. Bauer's eyes were wide, and he sat down dumbly on the bench.

"My God," he said.

Bauer's forehead was beaded in perspiration. The girl looked carefully, apprehensively, at him. He grabbed his suitcase from the rack and ran out the door. At the end of the corridor he opened the heavy, brass-handled door and threw out his suitcase. The train was beginning to move again, slowly, out of the lights, and then Bauer jumped.

*   *   *

The clock high in the Odeonsplatz read 11:15. Under the white arched lamps, young men and old women dodged the streetcars, making for home. Blue and white banners littered the roads. A French soldier leaned against a lamppost, ill, and all the while weary but dutiful policemen urged the dazed, smiling populace out of the square, into the narrow streets, toward the hotels and outlying districts of home.

A police car pulled up to the Hall of Justice and stopped. Steinman and Patrolman Koenig got out quickly, climbed the stone steps, and entered the huge, sculptured building.

The long hallway was dark, save for light spilling out of three frosted glass doors down the way. Steinman and Koenig walked quickly, their footsteps echoing hollowly. Steinman held up his hand for silence, and they stood outside the first office, listening.

"Once again, Frau Heder," said a precise, monotonous voice. "You did not get along with your husband?"

"That doesn't mean I killed him." Frau Heder answered in a dull, almost aggressive voice.

"He was aware of your relationship with this fellow, Nagle?"

"Of course not. I'm not stupid."

"Were your intentions to divorce your husband and marry Nagle?"

"No."

Steinman slowly opened the door. Frau Heder sat under a single suspended light. Olga Heder was a buxom, attractive, middle-aged woman. Out of range of the light, a silhouette of a man questioned her.

"After you and Nagle killed your husband, what did you do with the cleaver?"

"I didn't kill him."

"You mean your lover, Nagle, killed him."

"I have no idea. Better ask him."

Steinman closed the door quietly. "A cold fish, that one," he said. Steinman thought a moment. "Listen, Koenig. Stay here

19

for now. If something breaks, let me know. I will be in the other interrogation room."

Steinman walked quietly down the hall. He stood in the diffused light of the frosted glass. Again he listened carefully to two voices on the other side of the door.

". . . I didn't kill him."

"You were his wife's lover."

"Yes, but—I wouldn't kill for that. . . . What do you think I am?"

"You're a logical man, Nagle," Steinman said, as he opened the door and entered the room. The office was an exact duplicate of the first, save that under the suspended light Nagle, and not Frau Heder, sat before the desk. Nagle, a thin, sinewy man, nervously twisted his fingers through his tie, and looked up, frightened, at Steinman looming over him.

"That's what you are—a logical man," Steinman continued. "There was the woman, and there was Heder's money. You needed both—and the only way to get both was to kill the husband. You did what you had to do, simply and logically."

Nagle shook his head. "No . . . no," he stammered.

"Yes, Nagle." Steinman spoke softly, insistently. "And you did quite a good job of it, too. Have you seen the results of your handiwork?"

Nagle stared at Steinman.

"Hand me the pictures of Heder," Steinman said to the man behind the desk.

"Inspector Bauer has them."

Steinman stopped.

"Bauer?"

"Yes—he took them to his office."

"Inspector Bauer is in his office?"

"Yes, sir—right now."

Steinman pondered a moment, but could not figure it out.

"Continue," he said, and walked out the door.

A dry, monotonous voice began again. "Again, Nagle. After you killed Heder, what did you do with the cleaver?"

Before he could hear the answer, Steinman closed the door. He looked down the hall. At the end, light fell through a door over the tiled floor. Steinman approached, and heard from behind the frosted glass his superior, Martin Bauer.

"Is this Ludwigsburg? Operator? What? Oh, good. Yes. Hello . . . Dr. Rucker—I'm sorry to disturb you, Dr. Rucker, but I was given your name by Inspector Rodecker at Bonn. . . . Yes, Rodecker."

Steinman eased the door open. The photograph of the train station, smoothed and washed, lay on the desk corner. Steinman opened the door completely and watched Bauer on the telephone.

"No, Dr. Rucker. My name is Bauer. I'm with the Munich Police." Bauer now acknowledged Steinman, motioning him in with a wave of his hand, but to be quiet. "I'm sorry, Dr. Rucker, but I can't hear you. . . . Yes, a little louder, please."

Steinman walked up to the desk. On the desk were photographs of Heder, deceased, and some taken from before the murder, mostly of his face.

"That's much better, Dr. Rucker—I was told your agency has archives relating to the Nazi crimes. You do? Good. I'm particularly interested in picture evidence concerning the concentration camps."

Steinman slowly settled into a chair, eying Bauer.

"No. Pictures. Photographs of the camps, taken in the early 1940s." Bauer's eyebrows raised slightly. "Blank spots? I see. Where might I find such pictures?" Bauer quickly wrote the address. "Yes—yes—17, Rue Geoffrey—L'Asnier, Paris 4. Yes, I've got it—thank you. Thank you, Dr. Rucker." Bauer put down the receiver slowly. His face was clouded in thought. After a long silence, Steinman coughed.

"I thought I put you on a train to Kitzbühel," he said softly.

"I got off at the freight yards outside of town."

Bauer stood and picked up the photograph they had found in Heder's mouth.

"It suddenly became clear to me, about this picture. I don't know exactly what it means yet, but . . ." Bauer's eyes were excited, narrowed in thoughtfulness. He walked around the desk and thrust the photograph at Steinman.

"They're Jews, Paul," Bauer said. "They're at a concentration camp. Look at them. They're waiting. They're confused. It's in the feel of the picture."

Steinman sat unmoving.

"Don't you see it?" Bauer continued. "I remember these scenes. You must believe me. This photograph has that feel."

Steinman looked at the photograph for a long time. He dropped it back onto the desk. He brushed an imaginary speck from his pants leg.

"So?" he said finally. "This picture has reminded you of something. From the past, maybe. Is that a reason to jump off a train and come running back here?"

"Not reminded, Paul. This picture *is* a concentration camp. Those *are* Jews."

"I don't believe it."

Bauer handed Steinman an old portrait of Wolfgang Heder.

"Recognize him?" Bauer asked.

"Certainly. It's Wolfgang Heder, the victim."

"Does he remind you of anyone else?"

"No. Should he?"

"He reminded one of the ambulance attendants very much of . . . Hermann Goering." Steinman looked closely at the photograph. "And I agree," Bauer said.

A short burst of laughter escaped Steinman's lips.

"Oh, really—"

"Why not? A picture of a concentration camp. A victim who looks like Goering. I think it adds up to something."

"Martin, you—"

The door suddenly burst open and Koenig stuck his face into the room.

"Inspectors," he said eagerly. "Nagle has accused Frau Heder of the murder . . . and she is ready to confess—!"

Steinman dropped the photograph of Heder onto the desk. "Martin." He smiled. "Go to Kitzbühel. Climb a mountain."

*   *   *

Frau Heder was alternately laughing and crying hysterically. Bauer, Steinman, Koenig, the interrogator, and two uniformed policemen stood around her. The interrogator held before her a typewritten document.

"What does he say?!" Frau Heder laughed. "*I* chopped him up and lifted him—all hundred and twenty-three kilos of him— onto a hook?" An edge of terror crept into her laughter. "You believe it? You actually *believe* his lies?"

"Not entirely," Steinman said. "We're willing to listen to your side of the story."

Frau Heder threw the confession onto the floor, stood, and screamed. "There is no side!" Suddenly, her voice stopped. She looked around the room, at the men looking back at her, and, in appeal, her composure totally gone, whispered urgently to them. "There is no side! Don't you see he would say anything to save his own life? *He* killed my husband, *he did*—for the money— and now he tries to involve me—!" Frau Heder burst into tears, and sank slowly into her chair. "Don't you see?" She wept.

The shadows were motionless, falling out from the suspended light. Then Steinman moved his head almost imperceptibly toward Koenig.

"Get her some coffee," he whispered.

Bauer's expression was impossible to decipher. His gaze fixed itself on the woman weeping at the desk. Steinman took him by the arm.

"We'll have her part of the confession by morning," he said softly.

Steinman opened the door, and they stepped into the dark and dusty corridor. "Come," Steinman said. "I'll drive you back to the station."

"There are no further trains to Kitzbühel tonight."

"Well." Steinman grinned. "I can use your help, if you are willing, on a very special project."

In the room, in a circle of light, Koenig held a paper cup before Frau Heder, who sobbed, head in arms, while the other men had resumed their positions and waited patiently for her to regain her composure. Steinman quietly closed the door.

MUNICH:
The Second Day of Oktoberfest

CHAPTER THREE

The neighborhood was dark. Autumn leaves drifted slowly onto the sidewalks. A sense of impending mist curled through the trees. A blue Mercedes turned the far corner. Martin Bauer sat in his apartment high over the town, by the dark Isar, deep in thought.

The photograph, the resemblance of the butcher to Goering —a coincidence of events. Because of it, Bauer had jumped from a train, run back, and had made a fool of himself. He could have telegrammed from Kitzbühel, had he been so certain. Bauer knew that his intellect, that rare and delicate instrument, had gone wrong. But what if the instinct itself, after years of service, had failed? Bauer needed to know, but now he was too tired to think any more.

"Shhh," Steinman whispered. "Martin is asleep."

"So am I," said a woman's voice.

Steinman chuckled.

"No, you're not," he said. "You're drunk."

"I'm asleep," she mumbled.

Bauer opened his eyes. On the couch across from him a blond woman, her face delicately engraved with weariness, lay on Bauer's hat and coat. Her long legs, unstockinged, hung over the arm rest. She snored gently. At her feet plates of whiskey glasses and sandwiches tilted on the floor.

Steinman stood in the doorway, naked, leaning against the white doorjamb. Sparkles of light, reflected from a porcelain figurine, danced across his chest. A vague glow, from a back alley light, came through the bedroom drapes and outlined his hard, flat body.

Steinman looked over to the couch.

"Hey, Marlene," he said. "Wake up."

"Mmm."

"Everybody's awake but you," Steinman said.

"Go to sleep," Marlene murmured.

Steinman grinned again, and winked at Bauer. "A good girl," he said. He held up his hand in a sign of appreciation.

Bauer smiled, leaning forward and yawning.

"Yes. A wonderful creature."

Steinman observed his superior officer across the room. Bauer was brushing the thinning hair backward, and then looked for his shoes. Bauer thought too much, Steinman reflected. Steinman wondered if thought were the result of aging, or maybe the cause of it. He laughed suddenly.

"One of these days we'll invite Koenig to one of our projects."

Bauer pinched the bridge of his nose with forefinger and thumb, closing the vein, trying to clear his brain. Marlene and the alcohol, all the events of the night, had dulled him and then sensitized him, and his thoughts went crumbling against his will. Memories and images arose, appearing before him, meaning nothing.

"Don't think about it," Steinman said, sitting on the couch, covering himself with Bauer's coat, and stroking Marlene's leg. "You made a mistake. The whole world doesn't know about it."

"I just don't jump off trains, as a rule."

"Forget it."

"I don't act on impulse, do I?"

"No."

Bauer shook his head.

"I don't understand it."

Steinman poured a bit of whiskey into the remnants of ice in a glass on the floor.

"Here," Steinman said. "American whiskey. Let the peasants drink the beer."

"All right."

Steinman poured for himself. They drank in silence. A horn tooted in the quiet neighborhood, and then hoarse voices shouted out into the streets. A car squealed away.

"Oktoberfests scare me," Steinman said. "They get worse every year."

"They've always been a bad time."

"They kill, steal, lay around with other men's wives. It's terrible. They're animals."

"It's been worse."

The leaves rattled at the window, and a cold mist wandered freely into the room. Bauer held a black sock in his hand. Steinman was happy he had distracted Bauer's mind.

"I can close the window if it's cold for you," Steinman said.

Bauer nodded and shivered. He recalled, in that period before the Oktoberfest was reinstated, that men were shivering all around him. An unseasonable frost had come. Munich exhaled a frigid breath. All the trees, frosted over their green leaves, ex-

27

tended in great arcs along the centers and outskirts of town, and the great trains were lumbering along slick tracks.

"It's because Münchners were never civilized. Underneath, they're still in the Middle Ages." Steinman's voice droned on in the background of Bauer's thoughts.

Bauer remembered that soldiers lay then, shivering, on wooden boxes, wrapped in tattered coats and newspapers. Bauer avoided the misery in their eyes, and watched instead the wisps of snow blowing brightly up in the morning sun. With a great bellow of steam a train pulled slowly into the makeshift junction.

"Are the Americans coming?" Bauer had asked.

"How would I know?" said the soldier next to him. Bauer had recognized him from years before. They had been at the Police Academy together. Now he tried to wipe the frost away from his face. He stuffed the newspapers deeper into his boots. "Of course they're coming. What did you think—they wouldn't come?"

Over the ground the Christmas firs shook off their loads of snow. The freight cars pulled onto the sidings opposite, the animal breaths of men nearby steaming through fur and woolen scarves. Men and dogs stood around, and then the bombs fell, splitting the freight cars open. Rubble and timbers, clocks and signposts, all the innards of Munich came roaring out, and the men tumbled down into mounds of debris, and the fine-powdered snow rose gaily around it.

"Corporal," Bauer said.

"What is it?"

"Look."

The corporal looked with difficulty into the rising snow powder. An arm had disentangled itself from the timber and piping, and rolled itself down the heaps, the hand bent and making its way awkwardly down toward the tracks. Civilians and soldiers were slowly filing away from the debris. No one seemed to show any emotion. They only plodded along, flexing their hands for warmth and for reassurance that life still flowed within them.

Bauer put on his other sock.

"What?" Bauer said suddenly, realizing that Steinman had asked a question or had made an observation, and he hadn't heard.

Steinman shook his head and stood up. He stretched his long body, walked to the window, and looked out into the night. The colored leaves were growing sodden, as the neighborhood was drifting under a heavy mist. Water dripped unevenly from the trees. Over the darkened forms of homes the red signs of the Schwabing cafes glowed in the dark. Steinman reflected how beautiful the night was, in autumn, with Marlene and American whiskey over the dark Isar and Munich.

Bauer rose and joined Steinman at the window.

"You know, Paul, there was a time when they were shooting each other in the streets. After the war, I guarded the railroad tracks. We shot several looters every day."

"You think too much," Steinman said. "It's a bad habit."

Bauer smiled.

"Forget it," Steinman said. "Drink. Live. It's Oktoberfest."

A small snore emerged from the coat on the couch. Marlene turned over uncomfortably, her arms flopping across her eyes, trying to sleep in the unreal light of the Schwabing street lamps.

*   *   *

The fingers of fog swirled in tighter around the neighborhoods. Activity slowed, and soon the cobblestones glistened alone under the arc lamps hung from wires through the trees. A light rain had begun to fall. In the housing projects the East Germans, having been brought by the thousands after the fighting, celebrated the Oktoberfest, but with reserve, and now, predominately laborers, they slept heavily behind uncurtained windows. Through the alleys an old man came walking quickly, unshaven,

29

bent at the shoulders. The church towers of the Frauenkirche tolled the hour. The old man increased his speed, cutting through the construction yard and the back of the bakery, stepping quickly toward the housing projects.

Ernst Frisch was late. The garbage pickup was at dawn. They had caught him once with a bottle of gin in his pocket, and they had caught him again, sleeping in the basement. If they caught him late, he would live on the streets like a rat. East Germans, Frisch knew, were Prussian born, and Prussian they die. They assume control of the neighborhoods bit by bit, like Jews. Already Frisch, a native-born Bavarian, was reduced to keeping their furnaces going. He felt better when he climbed down the basement steps and closed the door behind him.

Frisch, at the age of fifty-three, had developed a deep distrust of most things. Only stone and steel gave him any sense of confidence. Expertly, he rolled barrels of ashes onto a wooden cart, and then bumped his way out, backward, into the night. The wheels bumped over the stone steps and echoed loudly. A sudden movement of the wind revealed a street light watching him from behind the leaves. Frisch had no idea what time it was. He hurried up the stairs.

Frisch had had no intention of celebrating the Oktoberfest at the pavilions or anywhere else, as crowds filled him with a strange anxiety. Still, he noticed that the East Germans sleeping in rows over his head had done so, and now he was the only one awake and working. Noisily, he rolled the ash barrels off the cart and set them with a clang into place beside the black iron railing.

Frisch stepped back down into the basement. He picked up a shovel and turned on the light inside. He closed the door.

The furnace was large and dark, lit only by the single bare bulb now dangling overhead. Shadows rolled on the walls. The furnace was made of brick, with three pipes below for ventilation, and grates in the sides and top. The curved roof was covered in a tarry, shingled substance as well as brick, and the mouth was bent into a lip, hammered down so that the ashes could be easily shoveled down into a waiting metal bucket. Frisch blew his nose raucously and blinked his eyes into the still warm glow of the furnace interior.

Heaps and small mounds glistened in iridescent reds and black. Suggestions of shapes still held. Frisch picked up the shovel and slid it through the unresisting, soft ashes. The mounds powdered down over the shovel. The metal scraped on cement. Frisch poured the ashes into the bucket. He did not know that the door had been opened. Frisch continued to shovel the ashes into the buckets.

Then a figure leaped on him. At first Frisch thought it was the Prussians. Then he felt a terrible feeling, and knew he was killed. He slipped on his blood, and slid on the floor, and shrieked a high, womanly shriek. Something horrible had smashed him. Hot liquid choked him. He groped on the floor. Something smashed at him again, and Frisch disintegrated into a dread, terrible darkness.

*   *   *

The furnace grew cold and sodden. Dark circles of rainwater gathered on the basement floor. By the wooden beams at the doorway fingers of blood had spread with the rising water. It lay on the surface, crusted. Under a blanket lay the charred and mangled corpse of Ernst Frisch.

"Give me a towel," Fischer said.

Bauer stood uncomfortably, staring at the circles of red and dark that absorbed through the blanket. Dr. Fischer knelt over the crumpled form, having pushed back the blanket. Rainwater had soaked through the shoulders of his black coat, staining down through the lapels.

"It was a heavy instrument," Fischer said. "Very sharp."

Overhead, in the public apartments, laborers not yet dressed, and aged, tired women in robes looked down on the police work below. Their faces were pale and blank as the windows. The fog came through the trees, bringing a strange smell of coal and tar. A cat paused in the alley, a foot raised, on the glistening asphalt.

"It was a cleaver, wasn't it?" Bauer said.

"Yes. I think so."

"Then it was the same man."

Bauer said nothing more. Then he shivered, and pulled his coat tighter around his shoulders.

"Multiple severings of the arteries . . . deep fractures . . . brain tissue . . ." Dr. Fischer spoke softly. Koenig, behind Bauer, wrote it down into a black pebbled notebook. ". . . lacerations over the right eye . . . separation of vertebrae . . ."

Bauer walked out onto the steps. He wiped his nose with a white handkerchief. The wind blew surface water down from the alley. Steinman, his tie badly mismatched in his urgency, stood watching him.

"Well," Bauer said, "I doubt very much Nagle crept out of jail last night to do this." Steinman flushed. "And I doubt Frau Heder has teams of henchmen running around to kill old janitors," Bauer said angrily. "It seems we have acquired a useless confession."

The assembled police stood in a semicircle around the doorway of the basement. Only the rainwater made a noise, falling off the landings overhead, running quickly down around the black iron railings. The men were cold in their boots, and their breath came out lightly in steam. They seemed to be waiting for something. Bauer looked out on the construction yard across the alley, the great yellow crane immobile, beaten now by the fog turned back into rain.

"Who found him?" Bauer said, in a lower voice.

"The garbage pickup," Steinman said.

"Interrogate them. Find out everything about Frisch. Find

out about his past—his political affiliations during the war. Understood?"

"Yes, sir," Steinman said. He wrapped his greatcoat around his legs and ducked through the rain quickly up the steps to the street level.

"Koenig."

"Sir."

"Interrogate the apartments. Find out who doesn't want to talk to you. Find out where the old man lived. And if he worked for the city, there's a picture of him someplace. I want it."

Koenig slid his plastic-covered hat over his large, ox-like head, and nodded. He went up the steps toward the apartments. Bauer thought a moment. Then he nodded to the photographer to begin, and stepped up to street level himself.

"Martin."

"Yes?"

Dr. Fischer joined Bauer, sliding his cleaned fingers into his fur-lined leather gloves.

"You must know that the assailant was very strong."

"What do you mean?"

"We had to pull the old man from inside the furnace. Normally, he wouldn't have fit inside."

Bauer paled.

"What's going on here? What kind of beast is this?"

Fischer shook his head.

"Somebody always breaks apart this time of year," Fischer said. "It happens."

"He was a poor old man. I know the kind. He lived alone, had no friends, no money, he went to play cards once a month. There's no reason to kill a man like that."

"I doubt reason has much to do with it, any more," Fischer said.

The cold drizzle seemed to fall on a thousand dark holes and hiding places in the construction yard and among the bushes

33

and alleys. Through the suburbs, on their way to work, or to the beer pavilions, a dozen suspects walked circumspectly out of range of the green lights revolving over the police cars.

Bauer raised a gloved hand. Inside the large blue vehicle the ambulance driver pushed his attendant awake, and the two of them emerged in yellow oilskin, carrying between them a folded wicker litter. Bauer watched them carry it down the basement steps.

"I don't like it, Karl," he said. "I don't like the look of it, and I don't like the feel of it."

Fischer and Bauer drew up the lengths of their coats and got into the patrol car. They closed the doors. A group of school children, carrying in their hands collages of autumn leaves, came jumping through the puddles. The patrol car started down the long glistening road toward the center of town, the green lights revolving impotently into the dull gray day.

PARIS:
The Third Day of Oktoberfest

CHAPTER FOUR

The rain followed Bauer to Paris.

There he looked down from his hotel window and saw the traffic running darkly through the boulevards. The old women who sold flowers on the street corners hid in their sheds. A misted damp came up from the sidewalks.

In the blocks of stone buildings men in white shirts looked sadly out from their fruit-juice stands. Africans dashed across the street, their coats draped over their shoulders. All the colors were dark and muted, and behind them all rose up the huge, Frankish, green church walls.

Two brutal murders, however, occupied the Chief Inspector's mind. He sat down on the edge of his bed. He turned on the bulbous lamp over the night table. Three photographs lay in a row on the bed. Wolfgang Heder, the train station with the waiting crowd, and now a grainy, ancient photograph of the dead janitor, Ernst Frisch.

Bauer looked them over a last time and put them into the inside pocket of his coat. He stood and put on the coat.

Bauer looked at himself in the mirror. He brushed back the thinning hair. He had the look of a man of public importance. The thick, sensitive lips, however, and the dark, withdrawn eyes betrayed a softer man within. Bauer wondered if he were not jeopardizing his career. He stepped back and examined his form in the gloomy light of the hotel room. He must be very, very careful in what he was doing. Then he left, and padded quickly down the carpeted stairs.

"To 17, Rue Geoffrey," Bauer said to the taxi driver.

The cab drove quickly through the city, raising water from the surfaces of the streets. Fluted columns, cafes, and roiling water in the gutters sped by. Bauer watched the massive cold green walls of the churches go by.

"Monsieur is new to Paris?"

But the Inspector had heard nothing. His hands tapped nervously on his pants leg, and he carefully touched the photographs inside his coat.

"Monsieur. We are arrived. The Old Jewish Quarter."

Bauer stepped out. It was a mausoleum. A block of building, flanking the muddy Seine, swollen and sucking at the banks. *Memorial to the Unknown Jewish Martyr*, it read in French. On the front wall were inscriptions in English and Hebrew.

The rain increased. A bronze cylinder in the courtyard—an urn—glistened with the water, as the rain beat down on it. Huge, white, and flat, the mausoleum extended four stories into the ground. A long hallway led down into the dark places below.

Bauer hesitated, then, with a gust of wind at his back, descended down into the crypt.

A young woman looked up.

"Welcome to the Hall of Remembrance," she said.

Bauer nodded, dripping water from his face and clothes. He followed her to speak to her, but she led him instead into the interior.

"There are six chests," she said softly, "which are built into the walls. Inside the chests are books in which are inscribed the names of the thousands."

The young woman paused, and waited for Bauer to reflect on that. She stood in the shadows. Bauer watched her a moment, and as he was about to speak, she said, "The crypt, in the form of the Star of David, contains the ashes of victims from the major concentration camps and from the Warsaw Rebellion."

Bauer stood a moment before the black, huge star on the floor. A low light shone onto the walls and the ceiling overhead. The silence was deathly.

"Look—see if there is suffering like mine," the young woman read.

Bauer looked at her slowly, the dark eyes and the hair of the young Jewess.

"That is what the Hebrew means," she said softly, looking at the inscription on the wall.

Bauer's eyes went to the Hebrew legend written over the black star. He began to feel decidedly uncomfortable. He walked up to the girl and, his voice echoing strangely in the darkened mausoleum, asked her, "Excuse me. The Center for Jewish Documentation?"

The girl paused a moment more, and slowly turned away from the crypt of ashes.

"You must go upstairs," she said, when she was at the door again. She smiled sympathetically. "Ask for Isaac Schneer."

"Yes, I know," Bauer said. "Thank you."

"You're welcome," she said, picking up her book at the desk. "Peace be unto you."

Bauer nodded awkwardly, and went quickly up the stairs. There he entered another huge room, this one lit by soft white

37

fluorescent squares in the ceiling. There was no one about. Bauer walked slowly into the room, watching the walls watching him.

"Hallo."

Bauer turned. From a small door an elderly man looked at him. The elderly man had a prominent forehead, and a small deformity of the back. He was smiling at Bauer. Bauer walked over to the man.

"Dr. Schneer?"

"Yes."

Bauer produced two letters of identification. "I am Chief Inspector Martin Bauer of the Munich Police Department." He gave Dr. Schneer time to examine his documents, but the old man only gazed pleasantly, directly, at Bauer. "I believe you can help me," Bauer said.

"Certainly. In any way I can. Please sit down."

Dr. Schneer stepped over to a percolator hidden among the books bound in metal rings and folders bound in dark brown ribbons.

"Can you have some coffee? We have so few visitors, and when they do come, it's always raining." Dr. Schneer laughed. "Please put your coat on the radiator."

Bauer sat before the desk.

"Well, then," Schneer said. "First of all, let us speak German, shall we? It will be easier for both of us." Schneer's German was impeccable, yet slightly stilted, as though he had learned it from a university. Schneer sat down, wiping away the coffee stains from the old wooden desk. He looked up.

"I must ask you, Inspector Bauer, do you represent your government?"

"No. Officially I am on leave."

"Oh?"

"A case . . . has interested me personally."

Behind the thick lenses, Schneer's eyes softened ever so slightly.

"You are looking for someone? A friend?"

"No. Not that."

"I doubt you are trying to locate a relative?"

"Dr. Schneer, I only meant that I am deeply involved in the case."

"I see."

Bauer thought he saw the blue eyes harden. However, Dr. Schneer continued to gaze at him with the same friendly, disinterested courtesy. Bauer began to feel uncomfortable. His hands fumbled as he took from his inner coat pocket the three photographs.

"I require certain information concerning these photographs," Bauer said. "I believe you may know them, or have them in your files."

Schneer accepted the photographs. He took off his glasses and held up the picture of Heder. The butcher's dour smile caught the light.

"A rather typical German face," Schneer said.

"Could it resemble a famous person of the past?"

Schneer looked at it again.

"Some infamous person of the past," Bauer suggested.

"Hermann Goering?"

"Precisely. Hermann Goering."

"Yes, there is a passing resemblance."

Bauer pushed forward the second of the photographs.

"What about this one?" Bauer asked.

Schneer picked up the photograph of the train siding.

"It does rather resemble a group of Jews at a train station. Mostly by the expression on their faces. A kind of . . . waiting. Disbelieving. Typical German clothes of thirty years ago."

Schneer looked up, and continued.

"But there are no badges, no guns, no guards, no signs or names anywhere. It could be just a coincidence of the photography."

39

Bauer's wet coat lying atop the radiator steamed and added humidity to the room. Bauer perspired freely. He sensed his mission was coming to a failure. Photo blowups of dying Jews affixed to the pale yellow walls around the room seemed to confront him personally now. Bauer passed his fingertips across his forehead.

"Dr. Schneer, if this *were* a concentration camp, and the Jews just disembarked from a train, which camp might it be?"

Schneer raised an eyebrow and re-examined the train siding.

"If such were the case," he said, thinking, "I would say, on account of this tower here, you see? A tower like that figures in many of the photographs of Auschwitz."

"Could you elaborate on that, Dr. Schneer?"

"Certainly. You see this ramp? There was one like it at the Auschwitz station, modified and enlarged in 1944, to accommodate more Jews. Rather typical German construction here, you see?"

"Yes," Bauer said weakly.

"But perhaps it is nothing of the sort. We have jumped to a conclusion."

"I understand that, Dr. Schneer."

Bauer nodded to the third photograph.

"Could you look at that one, please?"

Schneer squinted down at the large-grained picture of Ernst Frisch, which looked jauntily back at him. Frisch smiled with pointed, separated teeth. Frisch, before he was murdered, had been thin, with narrow, piercing eyes. Schneer shook his head.

"No idea?"

"None."

Schneer continued to examine the photograph of Frisch, but with no result.

"I'm sorry," Dr. Schneer finally said. The old man rose, the back bent at an angle, and he rubbed his eyes. "You know, Inspector, my memory has faded somewhat with the years. Faces blur or flee my mind altogether—a malady which has brought me great peace at times."

Bauer rose with him. Together they walked toward the door.

"I have an assistant, however, one who is writing a book. He retains an excellent memory."

Dr. Schneer indicated for Bauer to remain where he was. He put his head around the corner and spoke to someone down the hall.

"M. Picard," he said. "Would you come here, please?"

Footsteps sounded down the hallway. A small, dapper man, smiling nervously, appeared in the doorway. Bauer observed him carefully. The man seemed young, yet morbidly pale.

"M. Picard," Schneer said. "This is Inspector Bauer, from the Munich Police."

Picard's small hand gripped Bauer's, and the dark eyes fixed themselves onto Bauer's eyes.

"Inspector?" Picard said.

"Yes," Bauer said.

"Of Munich?" Picard said. Something in the tone of voice made Bauer even more uncomfortable. "The city of art and culture, is it not?"

"It has been called that," Bauer said.

Only now did Picard release Bauer's hand.

"Inspector Bauer needs to identify a photograph," Dr. Schneer said. "Do you perhaps know this face?"

Schneer held the photograph of Frisch in front of Picard. Self-consciously, Picard trained his memory upon the likeness. Bauer saw the small dark eyes go still and widen in recognition. But Picard handed back the photograph.

"Nothing?" Schneer said.

"Nothing," Picard said.

"You're certain?" Bauer said.

"Of course."

Dr. Schneer turned to Bauer.

"I'm sorry," he said. "Perhaps it will come to us. At the least, M. Picard can check for you through our Auschwitz files for pictures of the station. Perhaps one will closely resemble yours."

"Thank you," Bauer said. "I would be most indebted."

Dr. Schneer put on his long gray coat and picked up his umbrella.

"I must go now," he said. "Old age takes its toll, and I only work half days now. M. Picard will take care of you."

"Thank you again, Dr. Schneer."

Bauer gave a short, correct nod. Schneer observed it, and exchanged glances with Picard. Schneer mockingly returned the bow and readied his umbrella.

"Good day, Inspector," Schneer said, and left.

Picard went to the metal filing cabinets. Bauer watched the long fingers stride over the folders. Bauer approached, and caught a glimpse of the photographs: smokestacks, barbed wire over enclaves. Picard looked at him darkly.

"The light, monsieur."

"Excuse me," Bauer said, and moved away.

From where he stood Bauer saw the skeletal arms and legs moving quickly past Picard's fingers inside the metal filing cabinet. Bauer tried not to look, and at length Picard slammed shut the drawer with a sound that echoed through the memorial.

"You will see the resemblance," Picard said, and thrust into Bauer's face a photograph of a train siding.

"Yes, indeed. That is Auschwitz?"

"Auschwitz."

"If I may have a duplicate?"

"Certainly."

Picard went to a duplicating machine labeled xerox 4000 Convenience Copier. A hum rose from the machine.

"Who is that man?" Bauer said.

"Who, monsieur?"

"The man in the photograph."

"I do not know, monsieur."

"You do."

Picard said nothing, but abruptly reopened the file drawer and thrust into its place the original picture of the Auschwitz train siding and gave Bauer the duplicate. Picard's eyes fixed on Bauer again with the purest hatred Bauer had ever seen.

"I have said no, monsieur."

Bauer lost himself in the pools of darkness in the small man's eyes. A kind of magnetism held him there. Then Bauer left him to pick up his three photographs from the desk top and put them into his inner coat pocket, and he carried the coat on his arm.

"You would help me greatly, monsieur—"

"I will not help you, Inspector."

Bauer finally said nothing. He walked to the door, feeling Picard watching him. Bauer turned.

"Are your files open?"

"There is no duplicate of that face in our files."

Bauer looked across the tiles at the small man in the doorway of the office. Picard smiled strangely.

"You must go to Israel, Inspector."

"Israel?"

"Yes," Picard said, standing in the half shadow, his voice echoing through the mausoleum and the lights vibrating subtly off the walls. "The world archives are in Israel. With all the faces."

Bauer put on his coat, facing the bare white light of the doorway. He was conscious of Picard far behind him, and then he put on his hat, buttoned his coat, and stepped briskly up into the bright gray daylight again. Rain beat down over the dull traffic washing by all around him, and the noise engulfed him.

*   *   *

Miserably, Bauer tried to recall what had gone wrong. He had approached Picard incorrectly, and now the Paris archives were

43

closed to him. Yet Picard had known something about Frisch. Bauer was certain that he was right.

"Monsieur?"

Bauer looked up.

"Your coffee."

"Thank you."

Several Parisians sat under the dull red canopy of the outdoor cafe. The rain fell disconsolately from the awnings, onto the sidewalks, boulevards, and potted ferns. The street before the cafe was washed over with rippling clear water. The waiter mused over the scene.

"It's cold," the waiter said.

Bauer agreed.

"It's the Americans. They bring it with them. They bring everything bad with them," the waiter said.

Bauer nodded again.

"No pastry with your coffee?"

"No. Thank you."

The waiter left, and went back inside toward the kitchen and the other red-clothed tables.

Old men sat at the far tables, playing chess. They seemed to Bauer like the old Jews who inhabited the Schwabing cafes before the war, coming in from time to time to drink their strong coffee, with chessboards and newspapers under their arms.

"Monsieur would like something else?"

"No."

Bauer paid his bill and left.

He walked in an abating rain, down through the gray city, thinking. The street lamps had been turned on early, creating small luminescences in the fog. People walked slowly, darkly, over the bridges. Bauer walked until he felt himself become colder, clearheaded, and in control.

A train rumbled underneath his feet. He looked down and saw, below the bridge, the freight train clacketing along the shiny rails toward the switchyards, disappearing in the farthest curtain of mist. Bauer watched the heavy weight of the train press the rails into the earth, and the dark water ripple down off the switches on the ground. Bauer always knew why he had jumped off the train in Munich. And now the duplicate photograph in his pocket confirmed it.

He had been a soldier at the Russian front. They were coming back, at the end of that disastrous campaign. The men lay in the train compartment, packed like fish, bobbing and jerking with each motion of the train like broken marionettes.

Bauer had sat by a window, looking out, a young man, his cheeks not used to shaving. Suddenly a freight car, slatted and with steam escaping from the sides, went by in the same direction.

"Jews," someone had said. "Jews."

Bauer had not understood. Then the trains had slowed to a halt. In the blinding rain the fir trees shook off their water. Guards and railroad engineers walked among the ramps, through the mud. Across the yard the other train now rested, among isolated flatcars and mounds of coal on the ground.

"Look!" someone had shouted.

The freight cars had opened. Instead of cattle, people came out. They spilled out, their hands over their heads. They waited, uncertain, and then the guards prodded them down the ramps.

"Jews," someone had repeated.

Bauer looked around at the men in the compartment. They were unnaturally old, a darkness of death already in the eyes. Some looked down at the floor, spitting and coughing, others stared vacantly into space. Bauer turned back to the window. The Jews were already formed into a cortege, silently moving its way past the still, heavy flatcars, into the gangways and toward the distant towers.

"What is this?" Bauer had asked.

45

"They're going to the death camp, Birkenau," said a hoarse voice overhead.

"What do you say? A death camp?" Bauer had said. "It's a work camp! For munitions!"

The Captain had laughed a broken, bitter laugh, and everyone else had joined in. The train started to move. As the station slowly slid by, Bauer saw the name—*Auschwitz*.

*   *   *

Auschwitz, thought Bauer, an older man, standing on the high arching bridge in the fog. It was night now. The lights glistened on the sidewalks and the pavements.

Bauer realized that the case was throwing him back into memories he had long hoped were dead but now found were very much alive, and with disconcerting clarity. He had pulled down the window shade, he remembered. He had pulled it down and fastened it with its cord onto the lower shelf. What else was there he could have done?

Bauer walked back to his hotel. A despondency weighed upon him as he went up through the alleys in the mist. He sensed, rather than saw, cats roaming through the garbage and lettuce crates. The fog circled around the street corners. North Africans passed him, laughing.

That Frisch had been a Nazi, or resembled one, was no longer in doubt. Picard had given it away in spite of himself. There seemed to be a pattern, then, but there was no proof. Bauer needed proof.

He opened the door to his hotel. He walked upstairs and unlocked his door.

Bauer wondered how much money he had left. He sat on the edge of the bed and looked into his account book. It was not easy for him, but there was nothing else he could do. He removed his shoes and undressed. In the room the red lights from the street fitfully illuminated the walls. He lay down, resolved to do what he had to do.

As he lay there in the night, anxiety rolled up over him out of the dark. Even Picard seemed to be there, looking into his eyes, and speeding trains, and in that horrible nightmare, Heder, too, rose up out of his own blood with photographs in his hand. A streetcar squealed and woke up Bauer.

It was still night. Bauer looked up to the dark ceiling. He felt himself in a kind of well. He wondered if he knew exactly what it was he was going to risk. Bauer tried to close his eyes. He tried to sleep. But unwanted thoughts wrestled with him during the night.

47

ISRAEL:
The Fourth, Fifth and Sixth Days
of Oktoberfest

CHAPTER FIVE

"You will find Israel the most stimulating country on earth. I am not even Jewish, so I say it without prejudice."

Bauer thought the man looked Jewish anyway. The blue veins in the nose were prominent.

"Of course, everyone there is crazy," the man said. He laughed abruptly. "Maybe that is why I feel so much at home there."

Bauer smiled.

In the airplane, brilliant with sunshine, most of the passengers slept. Some few read their magazines or looked drowsily out the windows. Down below, on the shining surface of the Mediterranean Sea, an island was baking under the sun. Dust drifted up from the roads, and not a vehicle was in sight. The outlines of the island were white, in concentric lines of surf, beating around the shores.

"Of course, you can't blame them for being crazy, after what the Germans did to them," the man said.

Bauer looked up slowly at him. The man's eyes were closed, and the mouth set comfortably as he fell into a light sleep.

Under the wing of the airplane a long, low green strip rose out of the sea, and behind it trailed a long stretch of brown desert. The jet plane banked and came screaming down into Lod Airport. Suddenly Israel had come up, real and hot and busy in the Middle East.

Bauer felt himself peculiarly void of ideas. He stepped out onto the runway, carrying his handbag, and walked toward the Israeli soldiers who guarded the entrance ports. He wondered again if he should have come.

"How long will you stay in Israel?"

"Two days. Three days."

"Three days?— What will you see in only three days?"

"Yad Vashem."

"Three days? At Yad Vashem? What for?"

"I have business there."

The guard turned to the other soldiers. They spoke rapidly in Hebrew and then laughed.

"You will spend three whole days in Yad Vashem?" The guard put a hand over his heart. "I don't think you will enjoy that," he said.

The guard grinned, the white teeth shining under the handlebar mustache, and he handed Bauer's passport back to him.

"*Shalom,* Inspector."

So Martin Bauer entered the Israeli state. In his confusion he made his way through the small air terminal, pushing through the crowds which buffeted him on all sides. The police guided him toward a taxi, and he waited there, inside, beside a field of corn. When the taxi was filled by large men wearing skirts and a businessman in a fez, it pulled off down the road, and then crossed over to a major highway, and began the long, slow climb on the inland corridor toward Jerusalem.

Martin Bauer, his handbag in his lap, looked out on the Israeli countryside. Rows and rows of crops receded behind him, fanning out, and white, sun-drenched settlements appeared momentarily in the groves in the hills. As the air subtly cooled and the sky deepened its blue, the taxi began to climb through stands of trees. The hills, darkening in the glow of the sun, were rising snake-like in front of the Mediterranean.

The taxi driver said nothing, only listened to the radio. Two men in skirts discussed something in polite and agreeable tones of voices. Bauer watched the countryside. It had turned into that desiccated, dusty soil he had vaguely imagined was the Holy Land. The rows and rows of white rock turned into primitive dwellings, with sheep among the stones, caves among the hills, and then there were soldiers crowding the highway, and the desert lost its last trace of heat. On the edge of a great twilight, the first modern apartments arose, white as bone, up out of the edge of Jerusalem.

Bauer got out. The strange races carried their burdens in the streets, Europeans with their suitcases, and oriental Jews with bags of cement or wheat on straps over their forehead. Grocery stores were set into concrete square flats, and Jews, Orthodox Jews with black coats, black hats, and long braided hair, walked in groups down the dilapidated streets. Bauer stepped aside and let them pass. He stood a moment, suitcase in hand, watching them. Bauer was uncertain of what was going to happen to him.

Jewish soldiers went walking briskly down the streets, in uniform, submachine guns bouncing on their shoulders. Then the desert chill began to work its effects upon Bauer, and he made his way toward a large but moderate hotel.

Bauer entered the quiet lobby. With a sense of relief he saw German script on the newsstand. It was very still inside, and despite the chill in the air a black fan turned lazily overhead.

European ladies sat on the couches and chairs of the lobby, and Bauer cast his eye over at them as he entered. Bauer approached the desk. An elderly Jew looked up.

Bauer hesitated.

"Do you speak German?" he finally asked.

"As well as you do," the old man said.

"Excellent. I would need a room for two or three nights."

"Two or three nights. Very well."

The old man scrutinized his register. While he did so, Bauer looked at him. It was such an obvious Jewish face, the kind one draws on walls, with the bulbous nose and the round chin that sinks into the shoulders without a neck. It was the kind of face that used to come in through the doors of the Schwabing cafes looking for a chess partner.

The old man looked up at him.

"Is something wrong?"

"Excuse me."

"Room 27. The end of the hall."

Bauer walked down the long empty corridor. The last of the western glow threw its light up through the venetian blinds at the end of the hallway, grid marks streaking down the walls. It was incredibly still. Bauer had the fleeting impression that one could live here a long time, forever perhaps, in perfect peace.

Bauer unlocked the door. The room was reasonably modern, spare. The bathroom was of European design. It was cool and clean. With relief Bauer hefted his suitcase onto the bed and began removing his tie.

"Your radio, sir."

Without being asked in, the elderly desk clerk entered the room and set an old box-radio onto the night stand. He plugged it in.

"It's old, but it has good taste," he said.

"Tell me," Bauer asked. "What goes on in Jerusalem at night?"

The old man hesitated.

"Do you ask as Inspector or as private citizen?"

Bauer laughed.

"Night clubs, entertainments, things like that?"

"Ahh. Things like that."

The old man ambled to the window. He pushed back the soft red curtains and pointed down the road, through the foliage.

"You see down there Ben Yehuda Street and, following it, where it joins Herzl Street. You find there movie theaters, some cafes, girls, whatever you like."

Bauer looked out on the city. Brown, bricked walls snaked their way out of the white-rocked valleys, and behind their enclosure the domes and towers of Old Jerusalem. The stars were coming out over the palm trees. Trucks raised dust in rumbling past the enormous Jaffa Gate.

"And beyond?" Bauer asked.

"Beyond? You look at the holy center of the world, Inspector," the old man said. "On the right, outside the walls, you see Mount Zion. The Last Supper. King David is buried there. On the left your Christ was killed."

Bauer had the strange sensation of having witnessed this scene before. Perhaps it was from the Gothic engravings he had seen in the state museums.

"Where is Yad Vashem?" Bauer asked.

"Yad Vashem?"

"The Archives."

"I know what Yad Vashem is," the old man said. "You can't see it from here. It's in a tourist map in the night table."

Bauer smelled the distant, dry desert dust, and a touch of the grass that swept up the hills within the city. Sheep bells clanged lightly along the street, as the flock, not yet in sight, made its way up the road.

"Why would a distinguished man such as yourself go to Yad Vashem?"

"I have business there," Bauer said vaguely.

53

"Don't go there," the clerk said. "It's not good for you. Let the dead keep the dead."

"I have no choice."

"Then prepare yourself."

"I have."

The old man shrugged.

"As you must," he said. "Though I think it's better for you to buy leather in the Old City."

The old man left the room, moving quietly down the worn carpet outside in the hallway.

Bauer carefully washed his face and arms in cold water. A kind of dusty odor permeated the room. The sound of traffic, the deep rumble of lorries carrying broken stone past his window stimulated him.

The air was quite cold as Bauer stepped out. Moroccan youths sat on the railings, wearing lavender shirts and tight black pants. Crowds of European Jews came noisily in and out of the warm restaurants. Soldiers were running in and out, laughing loudly. He ate quickly in a noisy, crowded restaurant. The Inspector felt himself slipping, without his knowing it at first, into a void. Then he began to realize the obvious: that he was not prepared for Yad Vashem, and that in no way could he be.

He paid his bill and with a growing sense of dread walked slowly back to the silence of his hotel.

*　　*　　*

The morning traffic had stilled. The dust had resettled onto the street. The trees were motionless and it was hot. Only on the main street white-shirted officials walked into the huge sandstone buildings, past the armed guards. Bauer waited in the hot sunlight. Spirals of heat waves kicked up off the pavement and the roofs of the stone houses. At length a black car with a yellow checker around the windows drove up around a curve in the road and stopped in front of him. Bauer opened the door and got in.

"The Mount of Memory," he said.

The Inspector watched the flat roofs receding quickly behind him. His palms perspired on his black pants. It felt nevertheless cold to him. Moroccan children were playing in partially built courtyards, with small shovels and rags, brown in the hot sunlight. Over their heads the laborers were working on finishing their apartments. The sun was growing brilliantly white, almost a haze of pure white sky.

"Mister," said the taxi driver. "We are here."

High on the hill called the Mount of Memory there was a grove of trees, and the grove of trees was called the Grove of the Righteous Gentile, for on each tree was fastened the family name of someone who had sheltered Jews during the Catastrophe. Bauer walked down through this grove, the wind blowing through his hair.

His shadow passed among the shadows of the trees. High over Jerusalem other pilgrims joined him, come silently, sorrowfully toward the Memorial, and they all walked together through the grove. Bauer stood a moment.

Beyond the grove was the Memorial. It was a rough slab memorial on a stone courtyard, a simple, heavy hut. Soldiers stood beside it, as it caught the light shining over the Judaean hills. Bauer continued toward it.

There, beside and below the Memorial, was a low, white building. The Archives. The most complete center of information in the world concerning the Catastrophe. Bauer stood in front of it, in front of the white-rocked, heat-baked holy hills and plains. He touched the four photographs in his inner coat pocket.

Bauer went down, toward the small black opening, and went inside.

The Archives were well lit inside. Fluorescent lamps burned gently in the ceiling. A gentle hum of air conditioning sounded throughout the enormous rooms. The sunlight did not penetrate

Frank De Felitta

the rooms, only the soft, unchanging light of the lamps overhead illuminated the halls. At a far desk an old man bent over manuscripts, making notes in his own notebook.

Bauer walked down the rows of metal bookcases. Row upon row of volumes bound in plastic, manuscripts in leather, documents, stacked in shelves higher than his head. From where he was he could not see the end of the bookcases.

Photographs in leather pouches, with their titles in Hebrew, in Greek, in Russian, in German passed by over his head as he walked down through the rows. Bauer took off his hat. At the far end of the hall he met a young man in a white smock.

The young man looked up and smiled.

Bauer cleared his throat.

"With whom could I speak?"

"German? Just a minute, please."

The man disappeared. Bauer, standing with his hat in his hand under the white lights, began to perspire again. It was a cold kind of feeling. Then there were footsteps in the hall. The young man returned. With him was a stocky, white-haired man with powerful arms and chest. The man's blue eyes twinkled.

"I am Cohen."

"I am Martin Bauer—"

Bauer extended his papers.

"Please," Cohen said. "Come into the office."

They walked down the halls into the deepest interior of the Archives. The strength eroded from Bauer's legs. Cohen led him into a small office with maps on the wall and letters in Hebrew. The desk was incredibly cluttered.

"Please," Cohen said. "Remove your coat. You must learn to dress more coolly here."

Bauer listened to the German. It was the kind of German a man picks up on his own, a rough, street kind of German. Cohen prepared his coffee. At length he looked up.

"What do you want from the Archives?"

56

"I would like some information," Bauer said.

"Please."

Cohen indicated that they sit.

Bauer took from his inner coat pocket the photograph of Ernst Frisch.

"I need to know who this man is, if he had a Nazi past, or if he resembles someone who did."

"Why? You're not hunting war criminals?"

"No. The man was found dead in Munich last week. We think his death may be related to an alleged Nazi past."

Cohen raised an eyebrow. He finished his coffee.

"What makes you think so, Inspector?"

"Because another man was killed in the same way, and we know that he resembled a known Nazi figure."

"That is not much to go on," Cohen said.

"We found a photograph of Auschwitz junction on the first victim."

Cohen nodded. He poured himself another cup of coffee. He offered the Inspector a cup, but Bauer refused. Cohen reached for his pack of cigarettes on the desk and lit one, blowing out the match with the cigarette smoke.

"How do you know it was Auschwitz?" Cohen asked.

"I had it corroborated in Paris. At the Center for Jewish Documentation."

"Yes. Dr. Schneer."

Cohen leaned back.

"Well, our files are open, Inspector. I can personally help you, and I have a very good staff here."

"Thank you."

"It will take some time though, even if we limit the search to the Auschwitz files. There are thousands of photographs. Some of them are not clear. And time changes the way people look."

"I realize that."

"How much time do you have?"

"Two or three days."

Cohen shook his head.

"Impossible," Cohen said. "Do you have any idea how large these files are?"

"Quite large, I suspect—"

"Incredibly large. It could take weeks, months. And then you have so little to go on. A photograph of a man, and you don't know if he was at Auschwitz or only looks like somebody who was."

"I understand the difficulty, but we have nothing else to go on. The streets of Munich are full of thousands of people, drinking, dancing—it's the Oktoberfest there—and—"

"I know, Inspector," Cohen said. "I know Germany."

Cohen stood up, and Bauer rose with him. Bauer took up the photograph of Ernst Frisch. Cohen looked at him, and then rubbed his eyes.

"Well," Cohen said, "let us begin immediately. You will get the de luxe service, though I don't think you will find him in just three days."

Cohen beckoned to the young man in the white smock. The young man crossed the hall and entered the office. He smiled at Bauer. Cohen spoke to him rapidly in Hebrew, and the young man left.

"He is going to prepare the files for us," Cohen said, his back still turned against the Inspector. Then, slowly, he turned to face him.

"Tell me, Inspector. Why didn't you cable?"

"Excuse me?"

"Why did you come in person? You could have saved yourself time and money."

". . . I felt a personal need to come. I must satisfy myself."

"Remarkable," Cohen said. "You wanted to see Israel."

Cohen looked at him briefly and then left the office. Bauer followed.

They went slowly through the bookcases. The tilted volumes made dizzying patterns as they passed. Bauer had the distinct impression that they watched him go by. At the end of the first column of shelves, the young man in the white smock stood at a table, and in front of him were several leather pouches of photographs from the shelves. Certain documents, bearing photographs in the corners, were also set on the table.

"Inspector Bauer," Cohen said. "This is Laszlo Blackmann. He speaks little German, but I assure you his abilities are remarkable."

Blackmann smiled at Bauer and offered the Inspector a chair.

Cohen pulled the leather ribbons from the first of the pouches. Blackmann did the same. Bauer opened a packet.

"Are you certain you want to assist in the search?" Cohen said.

"Of course. Why not?"

"It is not easy."

"I am prepared."

"Well, I have seen prepared men go through this."

Cohen slid the contents of the first pouch onto the table. Boys wearing badges looked up at Bauer. Women, gaunt and naked, smiled out at him. In the background, fresh and rolling, were the undulations of the Polish countryside. Bauer began to look for a likeness to match the photograph of Ernst Frisch, now set in the center of the table for a reference.

Bauer turned to the second packet of photographs, each identified with place and names. The guard faces looked back at Bauer, grimly, over the barbed wire. They were faces Bauer knew well: the German faces—the ox, the horse, and the wolf. Indifferently, they mounted the ramparts with their rifles over their shoulders.

Bauer watched the slender wrist of the young man in the white smock speedily riffle through the photographs, stopping

59

now and then to compare a face to the photograph of Frisch on the center of the table.

Troop trains passed under belching smokestacks. Bauer became aware that both men were watching him watching the photographs. Bauer slowly looked up.

"You look a little pale, Inspector. Won't you step out for some fresh air?" Cohen said.

"Thank you," Bauer said.

Cohen showed the Inspector to the door. The bookcases weighed oppressively on him until he stepped completely out of the Archives into the hot air again.

Bauer felt hot and dry inside, as though a kind of fever burned in him. The wind smelled of sheep feces, and as the wind blew through the groves on the Mount, he heard the tourists, coughing and weeping, coming out of the great Memorial itself. Cohen remained by his side, silently smoking.

"Excuse me," Bauer said. "The photographs—there were so many—"

"Millions, Inspector," Cohen said. "Are you ready to go back?"

"Yes—I think so."

The afternoon degenerated into the last insanity of the Hitler years. Not the photographs alone, but voices from Bauer's own memories rose out of that mindless, murderous existence. Bauer watched the parade of gaunt faces, the exercises in the yard, the medical experiments, all those things he had heard about, read about, and convinced himself were not really true. There were thousands upon thousands, and he really believed he would have to be helped from his chair.

The scholars had gathered their notebooks and gone home. The fiction writers, too, carrying their notes and cards in filing boxes, had left the building. The activity in the Archives was lessening, and a small bit of slanted sunlight came in through the high hall windows. Only the three men remained.

"Listen, Inspector," Cohen said. "Blackmann has a good idea.

There is a woman on our staff who was at Auschwitz. She has a photographic memory. She is not supposed to work tomorrow. Maybe she can come. But even so I don't think you will find him in less than a month."

"I would be most indebted to you and your staff if she could help."

Bauer watched Cohen put the pouches back onto the shelves.

"In any case," Cohen said, "all you can do now is get some sleep and try to prepare yourself for tomorrow. We have barely scratched the surface."

Bauer nodded. He put on his hat; the perspiration on his neck had turned to an icy chill. As he walked toward the open door a cold wind blew down from the Memorial grove.

"*Shalom*, Inspector," Cohen called.

"Good evening, Herr Cohen."

Bauer wandered over into the grove of trees. He found himself walking up the inclined path, toward the darkness that was in the eastern skies over the city. Vague outlines of huge clouds rolled up over the desert hills, and he stumbled down toward the roadside and the waiting taxis at the gate.

*   *   *

In his dream the fields upon fields of Jews lay upon the ground, skeletons, and turned into water. Bauer was traveling across the countryside in a train. It was raining. As he looked out the window the wind kicked up swirls of water from the ditches and fields.

Bauer looked around the compartment at the familiar faces of the men in his company. They were wounded, all of them, their heads and hands jerking painfully as the train pounded its way across the flatlands of Poland.

"Where are we?" the Captain asked.

"Still in Poland, sir," Bauer replied.

Then the train came to a stop. Bauer watched the freight cars across the siding, the animal breaths steaming up from inside, through the wooden slats. The guards and dogs walked restlessly over the mud.

"Why don't we move?" the Captain muttered. He coughed a terrible cough.

Suddenly the freight cars opened and the skeletons emerged, wearing overcoats, and their hands were held over their heads. Bauer's head snapped back in surprise.

"Look!" Bauer shouted.

"Jews," the Captain coughed. "They're going to Birkenau, the death camp."

Bauer saw the cortege of skeletons trudging peaceably through the mud. The guards followed indifferently, prodding and pushing.

"What do you mean, 'death camp'?" Bauer said. "It's a work camp!"

The Captain snorted and blew his nose in a rag from his coat. He coughed his dying cough. Bauer watched the proud Germanic features twist into hatred.

"Death camp," the Captain muttered. "Death camp, death camp."

The train started to move again as Bauer slowly lowered the shade and fastened its cord onto the lower shelf. The rhythm of the wheels picked up underneath. Then it was quiet in the compartment again, and all the men only looked down at the floor, swaying with the movement of the train. They were on their way home to be bombed, and it was right that the Reich be bombed. It was right that Germany and all things German be destroyed. They were as good as skeletons already, huddled against the rain-spattered windows.

"No, no!" he shouted.

Bauer sat perspiring in bed, naked and cold. The light was pale and cold, a skeletal light; it was the false dawn through the hotel window. Dimly he heard the cries of Israeli children in the streets.

I was there, he thought, and shivered.

With wide staring eyes he sank back to the damp pillow. I was there, at Auschwitz, he thought. God, I was there. And I could do nothing.

Uncertain of whether he dreamt or not, he lay a number of hours on the bed. The light slowly changed, became brighter. Birds began to call. Finally there was a knock on the door.

"*Guten Morgen,*" said the old Jew, "*die Sonne scheint.*"

Bauer suddenly understood the accent: Yiddish.

"*Ja. Ja. Danke schön,*" Bauer answered.

The old man's footfalls died slowly down the hall.

With little sense of having slept, Bauer rose wearily, and washed his face, and then dressed. He put on his black suit once more and felt for the four photographs in the inner pocket of his coat.

Without eating he stepped into the bright morning, already grown hot. He waited on the dusty street corner. Jews passed him on all sides. The sun began to grow high over Jerusalem.

Then a black automobile turned a corner, raising dust, and the pedestrians scattered. The taxi came closer and stopped in front of him. Bauer leaned forward and opened the door. He sat down inside.

"Yad Vashem," Bauer said.

*   *   *

"Tauber," Cohen said.

"Who?"

"Tauber. He was an assistant *Rapportführer* at Auschwitz. He assisted Froelich, the man in charge of the gas chambers."

Cohen and Bauer walked down through the endless high files of photographs and documents. Maps rolled in tubes went by,

63

personal biographies, family histories. Their footsteps echoed ominously through the tiled halls.

"You know this for certain?" Bauer said.

"The woman I mentioned— She came this morning. She remembers the face. She identified him. We're looking for corroboration now."

"Her memory is reliable?"

"Faultless. Photographic."

Bauer was thinking rapidly among the volumes. He paused, and restrained Cohen with a light touch on the shoulder.

"Is it possible that the dead man *was* Tauber?" Bauer asked.

"No."

"Why not?"

"Because Tauber has been dead for twenty-eight years."

Cohen resumed his walking through the bookcases. His massive, leonine head looked straight ahead.

"Tauber was hanged at Nuremberg—after the trials."

Bauer watched the singularly handsome face of the Director. Cohen looked back at him while they were walking, without affection.

"The gods are watching you, Inspector."

"What do you mean?"

"I mean that normally it takes weeks to find such a resemblance," Cohen said. "And it has taken you no time at all."

They turned a corner. There, beside Blackmann, sorting through a leather packet of photographs, was a woman wearing a white sweater and a tweed skirt. Her long hair fell down over her forehead as she worked, and on her wrist dangled a gold Israeli bracelet.

"Inspector Bauer," Cohen said. "This is Miss Madeline Kress."

The Inspector drew himself erect.

"I am most grateful for your efforts, Miss Kress," he said.

She turned her head and looked up at him. She had the most extraordinarily clear gray eyes. Bauer saw that her expression had not changed, and that she looked at him with the same intensive scrutiny that studied the photographs. She smiled softly, and returned to look at her photographs.

"It will be a long day, Inspector," Cohen said. "If you would help us . . . ?"

"Of course."

Bauer sat down before the working table. Laszlo Blackmann handed him a leather pouch. Bauer rubbed his eyes a moment and then bent down and quickly untied the leather strings. Instantly he was swept by the same nausea that had swept over him the night before.

"Take off your coat, Inspector," Cohen said gently.

"Of course. Thank you."

"You'll torture yourself in this climate."

Bauer unbuttoned his dark suit jacket and folded it over the back of the adjoining chair. He loosened his tie somewhat and smoothed back his hair. He looked a moment at the corner of the table, and then down the endless white halls leading toward the door. Then he spread the pictures out onto the table in front of him.

Children with sunken eyes lay in heaps over the ground. The arms writhed along the pit markers, and the grim doctors went down the rows of the assembled Jews. Guards roamed through the lime pits, and in the background were mounds of Jews, bones and flesh, smoke and children's fingers.

Bauer could hardly touch the photographs. Men in pajama suits peered out at him, stacked in the bunks like chickens in a coop. Only their eyes were left, white under the cavities of their sockets. Bauer scanned them for four hours, looking for Frisch's counterpart, the assistant *Rapportführer,* Tauber. He scanned the Polish countryside, the German insignias, incoming trains, and belching smokestacks. Bauer passed his fingertips across his forehead.

Cohen touched him on the shoulder.

65

"Come on outside," Cohen said. "We can have some lunch."

The three men and Madeline Kress walked out beyond the doorway into the hot sun.

Over them on the Mount of Memory an American family came lightly down through the groves. The children went skipping down, but with a harsh word the father made them still.

Bauer barely saw, on a distant road, a military convoy snaking its way over the dry, hard hills. They raised a single line of dust blowing away in the wind. Beside the Memorial, another group of soldiers, relaxing, stood quietly at the dark doorway under the slab ceiling.

"You should go to the Memorial," Madeline said suddenly.

Bauer looked up.

"You mustn't be afraid."

Madeline Kress laughed lightly, yet her eyes were devoid of humor. Beside her Laszlo Blackmann ate his sandwiches, and also smiled. Cohen offered a sandwich to Bauer. Bauer refused.

"I was a foot soldier," Bauer said, almost conversationally. "In Russia."

Madeline and Blackmann continued to eat their sandwiches, as though they had not heard him. Their backs were turned to the Inspector.

"Have a smoke, Inspector," Cohen said, and offered a pack of Israeli cigarettes.

Bauer fumbled for one of the cigarettes. Cohen reached over and lit it for him. Bauer nodded his thanks.

"I was a private," Bauer said to Cohen. "Always the orders, you know. You had to obey."

Bauer felt somewhat better now. Although when the wind shifted in the leaves Bauer had a sudden image in his mind of bodies tangled in the ditches. Then the wind died, and as it passed away, Bauer felt better again. He smoked slowly, looking away from the two on the cement steps.

"Tell me, Inspector," said Blackmann, in slow German. "Would you like to stay here? In Israel?"

"No. I think not."

"You would prefer Germany?"

"I was born there."

"So was Madeline. But she lives here now."

The Inspector turned to the woman.

"Indeed? You are German?"

"She is Israeli," Blackmann said, smiling, squinting in the sun. He grinned broadly at the Inspector.

Cohen touched the Inspector on the shoulder. They went back through the shadowed door into the Archives.

The sheer volume of lives overwhelmed the Inspector. Bulldozers pushing fields of bodies. The scraps of their memories scrawled on edges of documents. "On edge of existence . . ." wrote one. "Mentally unbalanced . . ." "It is so easy to die," someone else wrote. "No one to help," wrote another. And on one shred of paper the Inspector read: "The beasts of the earth."

"Tauber!" Madeline said.

She threw a photograph down onto the table. It slid into the photograph of the dead janitor.

She rose and left the table. She went to the window, exhausted, breathing the bright, cleaner air. The Inspector looked down at the two photographs. There in front of him was an amazing likeness to the murdered janitor in Munich.

"A good likeness, Inspector," Cohen said.

"A very good likeness."

"Are you satisfied?"

Bauer stared at the photograph of Tauber—at the cocky, sharp-toothed face in the German insignia. Even the tilt of the head looked the same.

"A strange coincidence," Bauer said. "Yes. I am satisfied."

Bauer continued to look at the narrow, piercing eyes in both

67

of the photographs. Perhaps to someone in Munich there were other resemblances to other Nazis, long dead.

"May I have a copy of this photograph?" Bauer asked.

"Of course," Cohen replied.

Laszlo Blackmann and Madeline Kress began to replace the photographs in the leather pouches, and put the pouches back into their places on the shelves behind the Inspector. Then Blackmann left to assist an elderly man at the next table, who squinted painfully at columns of names in the manuscripts.

"I shall have it certified for you," Cohen said. "That this is Tauber, the date, and the place."

"I am most indebted, Director Cohen. It will bring the criminal to justice."

From behind the bookcases Madeline Kress stepped out, adjusting her white sweater over her shoulders.

"Do you think so, Inspector?" Madeline Kress asked.

"Yes. Why do you ask?"

"Because the Federal Republic normally elects its criminals to public office."

Bauer, fascinated by the depth of her gray eyes, remained immobile. Her eyes had the same imperturbable hatred as had Picard's in Paris.

"Let us hope for justice to all criminals, Miss Kress," the Inspector said at last.

Cohen led Bauer away, down the hall. In the office Cohen duplicated the photograph of the assistant *Rapportführer* for the Inspector. The two men stood in silence over the reproducing machine. They stood together and watched the light flash on underneath the rubber cover. Cohen slid out a perfect copy of the tilted, cocky face and handed it to Bauer.

"The Archives is not yet the place to find forgiveness, Inspector," Cohen said.

Bauer put the new photograph into the inner pocket of his

coat. Then he walked toward the open door into the late afternoon.

"*Shalom,* Inspector," Cohen said.

Bauer walked upon the Mount of Memory.

In the stone courtyard a group of tourists filed silently out from the stone slabs that roofed the Memorial. Bauer looked through the doorway. It was dark inside. His legs felt like cement. He hesitated at the doorway.

"Please move," a young woman said in English. "Others want to come, too."

The Inspector moved aside. He saw in the interior the tourists shuffling wordlessly around the darkened chamber. A kind of flame, a light, burned at the far end. Bauer stared inside but dared not enter. Then he bumped into an old man coming out, but the old man was bent and weeping, and did not notice.

"Either go in or out, please," someone said.

The Inspector nodded. In a kind of confusion, he entered the Memorial.

There in the semidarkness, a great silence reigned. Bauer was moved clockwise with the group reading names on the wall. The people gently, insistently pushed him on. Soon Bauer found himself in front of the light. Black iron grille and bricks and inside it a light burned, steadily, blinking gently over his face. Bauer's face grew warm, the eyes and mouth hot. He stepped back.

"Where is the synagogue?" asked an old woman in French.

Bauer turned to her, the sad, inquiring form. He shook his head. He stepped away. He noticed that his shiny black shoes stepped on the names of *Auschwitz. Dachau. Bergen-Belsen.* Inscribed into the floor. The Inspector backed away to the farthest wall. There no one saw him. Raising a hand to his face, the Inspector wept.

MUNICH:
The Seventh Day of Oktoberfest

CHAPTER SIX

The weather in Germany was phenomenally clear. The crowds lined the streets and pelted passing beer wagons with flowers. Suddenly out of a darkened portico, a woman ran, her costume slipping off.

"He's killing me!" she screamed. "Help me! Help me!"

But the crowd enclosed her and pushed her back. Men hooted, and old women tooted on horns. Just then an enormous man, a bear of a man, thrust himself into the middle of the crowd, and lifted the screaming woman high up, and set her on his shoulders. She laughed hysterically.

"He's a bear!" she yelled. "Let me down! Let me down!"

She beat ineffectually on the top of his head, and in her laughter, the tears rolled down her face, obscuring her red make-up. The huge man turned around and around, and she screamed in laughter once again. Dogs leaped and barked from underneath the resting hay wagons, and even the policemen grinned at the sight.

At that very moment yet another black-coated band tooted its way up through the old city, and ran into the crowd. The horns were shining in the sun, and the band leader held his baton erect, as the big man and his woman circled in time to the oom-pah-pah of the brass. Children squealed. The band leader held up his baton for silence.

"Husbands and wives, in Munich's fair weather,
You need but arrive and leave together;
Mismatches are rematched, at our autumn fair,
As with this naughty girl and her dancing bear!"

The crowd roared its approval. Smiling, bowing, tipping his little round black hat, and without missing a beat, the band leader concluded his improvisation and led his troop up the road, after the beer wagons, toward the never-ending activity in Therese's Meadow.

In the delirium induced by seven consecutive days of beer-laden celebration, the crowd danced and walked in crazy zig-zag patterns in the heat of the day. A line of children ran through the crowds, chopping at them with imaginary cleavers.

"I'm the cleaver killer!" they shouted. "Watch out! Here I come!"

The costumes merged into a brightly colored, involuting mass, and the noise rose loudly above the streets.

A window shut far over the scene.

It was quiet inside. The crowd danced silently below and shook its little streamers. The green hills of Germany undulated toward the haze of the Alpine slopes, and black birds flew over the endless green and yellow fields under the hot autumn sun. Colonel Schuckert looked down over the city and the landscape, and said nothing.

72

The Commissioner of the Munich Police Department was a huge, square man; the features of his face, however, were finely drawn. His beribboned Army uniform melded into his still tight and firm body as he walked behind the massive mahogany table in his large, high-ceilinged office and poured a small bit of amber brandy from a crystal decanter. He looked at the liquid a moment, then sipped it. The strongly etched face seemed cut from granite. It revealed no discernible emotion.

Behind him, on the desk, lay five photographs. In front of the desk, hat in his hand, stood Chief Inspector Martin Bauer.

The curtains hung still and heavy beside the windows. Not even the air seemed to move. The paneled walls were decorated in baroque figured heads, which now watched in silence the scene that played before them. Colonel Schuckert turned, and put a finger on the photograph of the butcher, Wolfgang Heder.

"This one is Goering," Colonel Schuckert said. "And this one," he said, pointing to the train sidings, "is . . . Auschwitz? And this man is—who is he again?"

Colonel Schuckert paused, and the silence was complete.

"Tauber, sir. An assistant *Rapportführer* at Auschwitz."

"Ah, yes, Tauber . . ."

Colonel Schuckert set down his brandy glass and sat down heavily.

"One of which you got in a museum in Paris?"

"Yes, sir."

"And the other one, from— Where did you get the other one from, Bauer?"

"From Israel, sir."

"Yes, I know."

Colonel Schuckert paused, folding his huge hands in front of his lips.

"Sit down," he said at last.

Bauer sat before the awesome desk. Colonel Schuckert pushed a button on a small console. The door opened behind Bauer

73

and a thin man in a dark suit, wearing glasses, carried in a file folder. Colonel Schuckert indicated, with a nod, that the folder be placed before him on the desk. The secretary did so, and stole a look at Bauer, and then quickly and silently left the room.

Bauer's eyes were fixed on Schuckert's expressionless face. The Colonel slowly opened the file folder and studied it. From time to time he nodded approvingly.

"Mmmmm," Colonel Schuckert said to himself. "Upper quarter at the Academy. Distinguished war record. Wounded at the Russian front—"

Colonel Schuckert looked up.

"Frostbite, sir. Both feet."

Schuckert's expression became pained.

"Ahh," he said. "Does it still bother you?"

"On occasion."

"What do you do for it?"

"I drink."

"Sensible, sensible."

Colonel Schuckert nodded approvingly again, and studied the folder. Finally he closed it.

"Well, now, Bauer. You're obviously not a fool. Shall we say that this time your judgment . . . was in error?"

"That's possible, sir. But I don't think so."

"Of course not, of course not."

Colonel Schuckert stood up with effort, and slowly faced the landscape out the window.

"I believe you mentioned something about a series of strange coincidences."

"Yes, sir. A series of coincidences which seem to establish a clear pattern."

"A clear pattern," Schuckert said. He pursed his lips. "Well, Bauer, let us examine this clear pattern in a reasonable and methodical manner, shall we?"

The Colonel began to pace the floor between the mahogany desk and the wall.

"Number one—you say that the two victims are linked by their resemblance to former Nazis, now dead. I disagree. Their faces are typical German faces. Our facial characteristics descend from a specific heredity. If these two men happen to slightly resemble Goering and this Tauber, then so do thousands of other Germans. As a people, we happen to look like each other."

Bauer dared not speak.

"Number two—" Colonel Schuckert said. He picked up the photographs of the Auschwitz depot and held them up. He continued to pace, without looking at them. "You say that this photograph was left by the murderer as some sort of protest against the horrors of the Nazis. I disagree. I say it was put in the victim's mouth by someone with a morbid mentality. I know these photographs. They are collected by the same sort of people who collect pornography."

Bauer sat in silence.

"Number three—" Colonel Schuckert turned to face Bauer. He leaned on the back of the massive leather chair. The voice became more direct and less distant. "Number three. We are halfway through the Oktoberfest—a time when people are drunk and excited. Inhibitions are dropped, and emotions range uncontrolled. Personal slights, imaginary hurts, kept tightly under check throughout the year, suddenly explode into violence. Not to mention those individuals on the borderlines of instability anyway. I needn't educate you, of all men, on the statistics of crime during the Oktoberfest."

Colonel Schuckert dropped the photographs back onto the desk. He slowly poured himself a small bit of brandy from the decanter, and drank it, looking distantly out the window once again.

"No, Bauer," he said. "Your clear pattern reduces itself to only one clear fact. A killer is in the streets of Munich wielding

Frank De Felitta

a cleaver against innocent people. And you won't stop him by conjuring up exotic theories and visits to God knows where."

Schuckert turned to Bauer again.

"Which reminds me. Who authorized your trips?"

"No one, sir. I was on leave."

"Well, your leave is canceled. Report back to your division for duty."

"Yes, sir."

Bauer stood and drew himself erect.

"And take these with you," Colonel Schuckert said, gesturing to the photographs.

Bauer gathered them together, and with a short, correct bow left the office quickly. After he had gone the Colonel looked at the door that Bauer had closed behind himself. The steely pinpoints in his eyes gradually relaxed and softened, and the Colonel shook his head and chuckled a slow, pitying laugh.

*   *   *

Colonel Schuckert's face was turned to stone. In the dark night his eyes stared, obsessed, and the high collar and the tall hat framed his head in the moonless dark. Blue lights rippled over the craggy face.

"Careful now. Lower him down!—" Karl-Heinz Fischer said.

Colonel Schuckert stood like a boulder against the costumed crowd. Jokes flew obscenely in the night air, men laughing coarsely and the women edging their way inward to look. The police lines were strained. Colonel Schuckert stood in the narrow alley entrance and stared down at the strapped and blanketed corpse on the ground.

"Get the wicker under the head!" Fischer barked. "Watch the head!"

Out from the blanket a small, pudgy face bobbed, still smiling in death. The spectacles still dangled from an ear. The blood

76

flowed down onto the attendant's cuffs, and as they lifted the litter the head and body tilted unnaturally.

Colonel Schuckert raised his fingers, and caught the attention of Bauer, coming out of the police car with Steinman. Bauer came over immediately. The two men stood in silence as the photographer made his flashes at angles into the impossibly narrow alleyway.

Schuckert leaned ever so slightly toward Bauer.

"Well, what do you think, Bauer?"

Softly, hesitantly, Bauer answered. "Well, sir, I think that there's more than a passing resemblance to—"

"Heinrich Himmler," Schuckert said, almost conversationally. "A gross boor. I loathed him and he knew it. He tried to have me transferred to the Russian front. But Von Rundstedt intervened. He hated Himmler as much as I did."

Karl-Heinz Fischer approached.

"Colonel Schuckert." Fischer nodded. "Good evening, Martin. I don't think I can tell you anything that you don't know. Except, perhaps, that he is becoming more adept with his cleaver."

Colonel Schuckert nodded. With a subtle signal, he indicated that Bauer alone should follow him. They walked into the dark of the alleyway, and there Schuckert stopped. Behind them, at the near end of the alley, the uniformed police tried in vain to disperse the happy, milling crowd in the yellow and blue lights.

Colonel Schuckert's breath was warm and pleasant, smelling of delicate plum brandies as he leaned forward to speak.

"Your theory, Bauer?" he said. "Does anyone in Germany know about it?"

"Only Steinman."

Colonel Schuckert's eye was strangely illumined from a distant lamplight. Bauer waited, saying nothing.

"Suppose it is true?" Schuckert said. "Who could this person be? And why now? Twenty-eight years after the fact?"

"I don't know, sir," Bauer replied.

"Well, say he was in prison all these years and he escaped. Or he is a veteran, and during the festival he broke down. Who? Who would do this? The left wing? The Arabs?"

Schuckert's eyes drifted toward the ambulance trying to push its way clear into the main street. The boys in the crowd pelted it with flowers. The siren began to wail. Schuckert, thinking heavily, turned slowly to Bauer.

"The Ministry will hear of this," Colonel Schuckert said. "Sooner or later the Ministry will become aware. Do you know what that means? And Bonn, Bauer. Bonn will hear of this."

Bauer watched his superior.

"If this line is pursued, it could mean my neck."

"I understand, sir."

"If I put you in complete charge of the case, how would you handle it?"

"I would give the case highest priority, and put more men into the field."

"Yes."

"Then, too, I'd seek help."

"Help? Whose help?"

". . . Israel's."

MUNICH:
The Eighth Day of Oktoberfest

CHAPTER SEVEN

As it had always been, Germany was a beautiful country. The long, deep green valleys deepened into the darker green of the forests. It was a country in which nature worshiped itself. The clouds rolled slowly over the Alps.

High in the clouds the airplane flew toward Munich. Voices inside were laughing, arguing cheerfully, growing excited. It was a clear day, unreal, as the copper domes of the Frauenkirche turned into view.

Deep in the back of the rows, Madeline Kress wondered why she had come back.

Below her, she saw the festival in progress, the diminutive banners hung on lines across the roads. People swarmed onto a fairground, numerous as ants. The meadows and towns grew larger, and the roads and farms grew nearer.

Then the jet began to scream, and Madeline Kress, after twenty-eight years as a refugee and Israeli citizen, touched down once again into the German state.

The pilots, grinning, came toward her out of the cockpit.

"*Sie bleiben hier?*" asked the blond one.

Madeline looked around, and saw that she was the last to rise from her seat. She took up her small handbag and went out onto the runway apron, feeling the beat of her pulse.

Inside the shuttle bus a fat German man swayed heavily with the turns. He breathed on her.

"*Entschuldigung,*" he said.

German faces, German types of faces, eyed her. They looked at her clothes, her Israeli handbag, and looked up at her German face. At the passport control the guards looked at her closely.

"How long will you stay in the Federal Republic?"

"Several days. A week."

The guard smiled at her eyes, her mouth, her breasts. "*Guten Tag, Fräulein.*"

The Germans pressed in upon her. The escalator was crowded. It stopped momentarily. The assembled mass moved sluggishly, the rear piling into the stalled front. Madeline felt her face perspiring.

"*Rudi! Rudi!*" called a hysterical mother. "*Wo bist du?*"

But the guards pushed the crowds on to the next platform. Madeline came out to the level of the great hall. There the red neon signs flashed over the dark-clothed masses, screaming their warnings and messages in Germanic print.

Nur Eintritt!

Ausgang!

Zu den Badenzimmern—Frauen!

Policemen looked at her from across the crowd. Madeline saw the one nudge the other and point to her. They began to move through the crowd in her direction. Madeline's heart pounded.

"Der Express nach Nürnberg, Bayreuth, und Berlin ist jetzt auf Gleis nummer sieben!" boomed the loudspeaker in crisp, sudden German.

The two policemen approached closer. Madeline saw that with them was a man in a black coat. Just then the shuttle service from Augsburg arrived, and a new stream of people swarmed into the great hall. Bodies pushed in all directions. The noise of the crowd rose. Soldiers came forward suddenly and embraced their wives behind the lines. Women squealed.

"Fräulein!" waved the policemen.

Rooted, unable to move, Madeline saw them come closer, pushing their way through the crowd. The uniformed policeman reached for her handbag. The man in the black coat shouted at her, above the noise—a badge shone in front of her face—

Madeline felt herself dropping into dark space. She fell forward and felt her body fall. Then she felt nothing. . . .

She lay on a bench in the airport restaurant. Over her was the heavy black coat. Under her head was the bundled coat of a uniformed policeman. Gradually the voices became distinct to her. She opened her eyes on the bright lights overhead. She tried to rise, but the Inspector gently restrained her.

"Not yet," Bauer said. "Rest awhile."

Madeline pushed away his hand. She sat up uncertainly.

The Inspector handed her a cup of steaming hot tea, which she took in her hand. She sipped gingerly from it. She avoided his gaze. Then she brushed aside her long brown hair and tried to stand.

"The pressure changes," the Inspector said, rising with her. "It often happens."

She handed him back the cup of tea, and tucked her blouse

81

into her skirt. Embarrassed, she looked for her handbag. Koenig promptly gave it to her.

"Well," she said. "I am not a weakling."

"Of course not," Bauer said. "And I, for my part, must apologize for not meeting you at the gate. The traffic, you know, this time of year—"

"Yes. I know. Can we go, Inspector?"

Bauer offered her his arm, but she walked instead behind him.

"Are you well enough to walk to the car?"

"Of course."

"Excellent," the Inspector said.

Bauer, Koenig, and Madeline Kress walked out to the parking ramps. From time to time Bauer turned and smiled protectively at her. Madeline did not notice him, but looked guardedly around at her first view of the German state.

Koenig opened the door. Madeline sat uncomfortably in the back seat. The Inspector sat beside her. Koenig drove toward the interior of Munich. The houses on the outskirts flew by, and the small yards, and the geese along the roadside. Madeline watched with wide, open eyes. She sensed the Inspector next to her.

"Why are you looking at me?" Madeline said.

"Forgive me," Bauer said.

Bauer ignored the look of Koenig in the rear-view mirror. He looked out the window. At length he turned to her again. He spoke softly.

"Your arrival causes me some confusion," Bauer said.

"Why?"

"I had expected Director Cohen to come, or even Blackmann, when I cabled."

"And now?"

"Miss Kress, it is the Oktoberfest. There is not a spare room for forty kilometers. Not a hotel, pension, or church basement."

Bauer thought rapidly as the countryside continued to meld

into the rectilinear blocks of the new city. The ride, which normally gave him pleasure, now filled him with foreboding.

"Would you stay at my apartment, while I stay with another Inspector?"

"Of course. Why not?"

"It is not exactly the Sheraton Hotel."

"I am not used to luxury."

"Excellent," was all Bauer could think of to say. He remained turned away, and faced the inner city of Munich growing tall around them. The ancient gargoyles, streaked with rain deposits, regarded them with amusement as they passed by.

As they drove through the central city, the twin copper towers looked down on them, and the profusion of costumed pedestrians and blue streetcars made way for them.

"Where is the synagogue?" Madeline suddenly said.

"Excuse me?"

"There was a synagogue here."

"I don't understand," Bauer said.

"There," Madeline said, pointing out the window. "There, where that fountain is, there was once the old synagogue."

Bauer followed her finger. There, over a white pool, a bronze Moses held a rod over the rock, and a thin stream of water arched down into the bottom of the fountain. Bauer followed the sculpture with his eyes down to the base, and then he looked back at the disappointed face of the Israeli woman.

"It's true," he said. "They burned it. I had forgotten."

They drove in stony silence through Munich. From time to time Madeline looked carefully at a passing house, or a church streaked in mineral deposits. Some kind of emotion seemed to be troubling her face, something Bauer had not yet seen. However, she said nothing. The afternoon had faded, and the lights were coming on all over the town. Families in the residential districts were making their way toward the fairgrounds. Koenig

83

Frank De Felitta

drove carefully, and stopped beside the white apartment building along the banks of the Isar.

"Please follow me," Bauer said.

Bauer walked up the sidewalk and Madeline followed, still carrying her own handbag.

"As I said, it is nothing special," Bauer said, and he unlocked the outer door. Inside the hall, mirrors reflected their images as they stood together, and they walked down the carpet toward Bauer's door. A peculiar wan light bathed the inner hall. He opened the private door.

Bauer's sweater, a number of dishes, and an opened book lay on the floor. The bedroom, discernible beyond an opened door, was not made up. A bottle of whiskey was visible on the far dresser.

Bauer walked quickly into the bedroom and began clearing the room. He stripped the linen from the bed. Then he came out, carrying a number of magazines and empty coffee cups in his arms.

"Please," he said. "Come in. It is getting cold."

The Inspector cleaned his kitchen and changed the linen in the bathroom. There was the sound of his working. He took all things from the living-room floor and placed them properly.

"It looks a bit better, doesn't it?" he said, embarrassed.

Madeline remained in the open doorway, still holding her handbag. She still said nothing, and watched him, oddly. Bauer pulled out a chair in the kitchen and gestured for her to sit down.

"Coffee, Fräulein Kress?"

Madeline shook her head.

"Are you afraid to be here?" he asked.

Madeline shook her head again.

"Not afraid, Inspector. The feeling is much different."

"I understand."

"I don't think so."

84

Bauer offered to her his silver cigarette case, but she made no sign, and so he returned it to his pocket unopened.

"From Yad Vashem I know your abilities," he said. "I hope our work together here will be equally as fruitful."

"I hope so, Inspector."

"Your German, in any case, is very good." He smiled.

There was no response.

"You know," he said, "since I was at Yad Vashem, my mind has been full of these strange thoughts—"

"I am not interested, Inspector."

Bauer stopped.

"If you have some comments to make, write a book. I am not interested."

Bauer smiled. "You are a hard person, Miss Kress."

"I am not hard," she said. "I have a good memory."

The Inspector sighed and rose from the table.

"Here are my keys," he said. "There are no others to the building. You will find my telephone numbers on the table. Tonight I will be at the Justice Building."

"At night, Inspector?"

"Yes. Two nights ago, another man was murdered. With a long, heavy butcher's cleaver. Stuffed into an alley. That is why I was authorized to cable for you."

"Was he a Nazi?"

"No, Miss Kress. A bookkeeper. He happened to look like Heinrich Himmler."

Madeline looked at him ironically yet curiously.

"Someone is going around killing Nazis?"

"Germans who look like Nazis."

"A subtle distinction, Inspector."

The Inspector took from his cigarette case a filter cigarette and nervously put it into his mouth. Some kind of undefined agitation worked its way onto his face. Nevertheless, he strove to control it.

"It will not be pleasant work, Miss Kress," he said, "any more than it was for me at Yad Vashem. However, I am grateful that you came. If you care for dinner, I will be happy to come by for you."

"Thank you, no. I am just tired."

"Then I suggest that you get as much sleep as you can."

Bauer adjusted his small, black hat onto his head and smoothed down the sides of his hair.

"Good evening, Miss Kress."

Bauer, who thought he had left those feelings in the Israeli archives, now walked down the darkened halls with a familiar sense of dread. He opened the outer door and walked out under the stars to where Koenig patiently listened to the radio in the patrol car.

"Turn it off, please," Bauer said.

He sat in the patrol car and Koenig drove off toward Steinman's apartment, where Bauer would spend the nights. Bauer watched the autumn leaves passing overhead. He was weary in his bones. He felt himself withdrawing into a deep and ominous gloom. The homes and gabled churches flew past them, and memories of Madeline's eyes, like Picard's, remained in Bauer's mind, as the black shadows of trees passed over him.

*   *   *

Alone in the Inspector's rooms, Madeline Kress still sat at the kitchen table. She cautiously turned on another light and stepped into the living room. The furniture oppressed her there, with its heavy, German orderliness.

She went into the bedroom. It, too, was so orderly, so regular, and so lifeless. It hung heavily and dead all around her.

On the dresser were his artifacts—his pipes, his framed photographs, and a small chess set. Madeline walked over and looked at the photographs. There, on the porch of a mountain chalet, an elderly couple smiled gently into the sunlight. Beside the photograph was a glass bowl full of foreign coins, and stamps of Europe. In a framed portrait, a long-legged girl named Marlene smiled coyly down from a stool. She looked so very chic, so very fashionable, so European. Madeline picked up the portrait and studied it.

Behind it was another photograph. Young Inspector Bauer stood in a cornfield and smiled. The wind blew through his hair. He wore the neat, clean uniform of the Wehrmacht.

She backed away. She went back into the living room and closed the bedroom door. She undressed and lay under her sweater on the couch, feeling a strange, unpleasant weariness.

In the dim light of the German police officer's apartment, Madeline Kress wondered if she had made a terrible mistake.

After a long while, she got up and went into the bedroom. She removed the blankets from the bed and took them back into the living room. She spread them over the couch. Then she lay down under them. Immediately, that strange weariness, dreadful, tugged at her to go to sleep.

As a feather falls from a bird in flight, softly, undulating against the mysterious currents that rise up against it, so Madeline, slipping from consciousness, now fell into time and floated backward into the darkness.

The Isar tumbled. A blue river bubbling over its stones, the Isar shivered up a mist which tingled Madeline's nose. A youthful Madeline stood on the cobblestone walk behind her mother's house. There was a basket under her arm. The ringlets of her hair hung lightly at her ears. On her way to the baker's, she had paused a moment to listen to her mother's clear soprano voice emanating from somewhere within the house. Transfixed, Madeline stared at the bubbling blue Isar and listened to the sad, autumnal song of her mother. The chill in the autumn air, and the jumbling, swirling Isar under the cobbled walks always made her think of her mother. Her mother, and the musical evenings.

Madeline was eight. It was summertime and the house was festive. Joyful. All the finest Jews of Munich had gathered there. Under the bright chandeliers the wit and laughter rang out; her mother sat at the piano. A soulful, dark woman, she sat with a distant smile and played Chopin. The admiration was evident in all men's eyes as she played. It was a sweet, sad melody she played, and Madeline watched her shyly from the corner of the room. There was a great peace in the room. Then, for an encore, Madeline, encouraged by gentle smiles and loving applause, would accompany her mother on her violin, and together they would round out the evening in a Schubert "Seranata," or a lilting Strauss waltz. At the conclusion, with the echo of the final cadence dying away, applause and wit and laughter would again fill the festive rooms, and Madeline, holding her mother's hand, would truly feel she had become a part of some private, unapproachable area of her mother's soul.

And then, one day, alone in her room, Madeline looked out of the window. It was autumn again, and under the brooding Alps, dimly visible in a curtain of blue mist, stood a tall wheat field where the countryside came up to the city. It was a golden field, wavering in the morning freshets. It was a vision of impossible beauty, Madeline had thought, and when she heard her mother downstairs laughing with her father, she realized that she did not ever want to leave this Germany. But over the ridges of the wheat fields came men in dark silhouette, came men in unison, wielding scythes, distantly and methodically.

The Einsatz unit would enter a village or town and order the prominent Jewish citizens to call together all Jews for the purpose of "re-settlement." They were requested to hand over their valuables and to surrender their outer clothing. They were transported to the place of execution in trucks and trains—always only as many as could be executed immediately. In this way an attempt was made to keep the span of time from the mo-

ment in which the victims knew what was about to happen to them until the time of their execution as short as possible.

Hiding under a kitchen table, given a dirty crust of bread to eat by her benefactress, the cook, Madeline peered out of the window. The Auschwitz compound was crossed by lines of Jews, some heading for the barracks, others for the pits. The sun beat down on the machine guns. The pits filled with jerking victims. They all died alike, shivering now and then in a last convulsion. Polish peasant and Munich pianist, all alike. Madeline, watching from the high corner of the cook's window, wondered which group had died with her mother.

TO THE CENTRAL CONSTRUCTION OFFICE OF THE SS AND POLICE, AUSCHWITZ:

SUBJECT: Crematoria 2 and 3 for the camp.
We acknowledge receipt of your order for five triple furnaces, including two electric elevators for raising the corpses and one emergency elevator. A practical installation for stoking coal was also ordered and one for transporting ashes.
We guarantee the effectiveness of the cremation ovens as well as their durability, the use of the best material, and our faultless workmanship.
Awaiting your further word, we will be at your service.

Heil Hitler!
C. H. KORI, G.M.B.H.

Madeline waited in the barracks with the other children. They had been assembled the night before, and had been fed twice. This puzzled them greatly for, as one boy said, if they were meant to die with the others, they would not have been fed. Outside, visible through the grimy window, the lines of newly arrived Jews moved sheep-like in single file to the bathhouses. But Madeline knew they were not bathhouses. The sweet-sour smells of burning flesh hung over the compound when the breezes did not blow. Madeline wondered when she was going to die. And why she had not died already.

Still another improvement we made over Treblinka was that at Treblinka the victims almost always knew that they were to be exterminated, while at Auschwitz we endeavored to fool the victims into thinking that they were to go through a delousing process.

When the trains would arrive, what would the victims see? Well-kept lawns with flower borders; the signs at the entrances saying BATHS. The unsuspecting Jews thought they were being taken for a delousing bath, to the accompaniment of gay music. For, greeting them, was an orchestra of young, pretty children, which we formed from among the inmates, who played gay tunes from The Merry Widow *while the selections were being made.*

So Madeline lived. She lived because she could play the violin.

The night-lights swept the inner barracks walls. Their only meal that day had consisted of bread and turnips. They were being fed less frequently now, which worried Madeline. But not David, the flutist. As usual, he had an answer. "The war is going badly for them. They have less food," he explained, whispering across the room from the boys' side of the barracks. Snug and warm between clean sheets, Madeline watched the tiny shadows of the night-lights flee across the shelf-beds and jump into the darkness. It occurred at twenty-second intervals. Across the compound she could hear women whimpering, a few coughing. Her mother was dead now, she was sure of that. Her father, though, might still be alive, working, perhaps. Madeline listened to the sounds of the guards outside. They laughed about the Jewish "band" girls. Madeline wondered what was going to happen to them all. And when they would be killed.

But the years passed, and the band played on. The trains

came, spilled out their doomed cargoes to the strains of *Vienna Woods*. Men from Munich came, one who remembered her parents. He asked about Poland. She asked about Germany. Everywhere it was the same: it was true. The Jews were being exterminated. In a year there would not be a Jew alive on the earth.

"Another improvement we made over Treblinka was that we built our gas chambers to accommodate two thousand people at one time, whereas at Treblinka their gas chambers only accommodated two hundred people each."

But Madeline knew that not all Jews died in the bathhouses. Men were experimented upon. Their genitals were removed, or transformed. Men were sealed in airtight chambers and the air was removed. Men were plunged into icy baths for days, weeks, until they became insane and died. Women were experimented upon. Artificial inseminations. Operations upon the breasts. Women who were pregnant were aborted in a variety of ways. Tattoos, amputations, used for the enjoyment of the guards. Children were experimented upon. Boxcars filled with children's shoes were found after the war.

. . . I also want to talk to you quite frankly on a very grave matter. Among ourselves it should be mentioned quite frankly, and yet we will never speak of it publicly . . .

I mean . . . the extermination of the Jewish race . . . Most of you must know what it means when one hundred corpses are lying side by side, or five hundred, or one thousand. To have stuck it out and at the same time—apart from exceptions caused by human weakness—to have remained decent fellows, that is what has made us hard. This is a page of glory in our history which has never been written and is never to be written. . . .

Madeline wondered not if there were a God, for manifestly there was none. She wondered not if there were no humanity, for equally manifest was it that there was none. She wondered only when there would be an end to it.

And then the day came when the music stopped. When Madeline found herself confronted by soldiers wearing strange uniforms and speaking of freedom. And even though it seemed true, for all the scarecrows in pajamas came gaunt and hollow-eyed out of the barracks and mingled freely with the soldiers, Madeline felt only deprived that she had not joined the others in the pits.

For all those who died, all those lovely men and women of wit and laughter, there was only a handful left; vague fleeting images whom, now, for all her iron discipline, Madeline could not, even in dreams, will to come alive again.

The old familiar smells of the Munich night wafted in through Madeline's open window. A gentle breeze, bringing an aura of late autumn, and the fine dust from colored leaves, and the coolness of country fields which bordered the twinkling Isar. It was a fine, peaceful, tantalizing smell. Madeline stirred uneasily on the couch in Inspector Bauer's apartment.

MUNICH:
The Ninth Day of Oktoberfest

CHAPTER EIGHT

The District Attorney was a man who never lost his temper or his poise. He smiled from time to time, when he was angry, or he drummed his fingers, but he was always in firm control of himself. His name was Hugo Flanck, a slight, lean man, with a small head set uncertainly onto its small neck. Now he sat at the head of his long conference table, smiling and drumming his fingers.

The room was simple and functional, devoid of windows and ornamentation. Along one side of the table were seated Chief Inspector Martin Bauer and Inspector Paul Steinman. The large body of Colonel Schuckert sat across from them. The District Attorney, however, directed his gaze down the length of the table. There the woman with the startling gray eyes pulled photographs from a stack, one by one.

"Ernst Kaltenbrunner," Madeline said. She spoke in a flat, emotionless voice. "SS police leader—Heydrich's replacement. Hanged, Nuremburg, 16 October 1946."

The photograph of Ernst Kaltenbrunner was passed to Colonel Schuckert, who examined it, and from there to Chief Inspector Bauer, who then gave it to Inspector Steinman. District Attorney Flanck pushed it quickly aside.

"Martin Bormann—Chief of Party Office from May 1941," Madeline said. "Hitler's personal secretary. Last seen alive 2 May 1945. Fate unknown."

The photograph of Martin Bormann was passed to Colonel Schuckert, who studied it and nodded approvingly. The Colonel reached across the table and handed it to Inspector Bauer. Steinman studied it over the shoulder of Bauer, then pushed it down the table to the District Attorney. Flanck's drumming fingers pushed the photograph away, on top of the picture of Ernst Kaltenbrunner.

"Alfred Rosenberg—Chief of Foreign Political Section in Party Office. Hanged Nuremburg, 16 October 1946."

When the photograph of Alfred Rosenberg reached Flanck, the drumming fingers slapped it down with a snap that echoed in the pale featureless room. Flanck smiled, but his eyes contained no humor.

"Haven't we had enough of this?" Flanck asked.

It was silent in the room; only the air purifier made any noise at all. Flanck was motionless and waited for an answer. Colonel Schuckert eyed him carefully.

"Not quite," Colonel Schuckert said.

The District Attorney softened his voice.

"You believe this nonsense, Colonel?"

Colonel Schuckert held in front of him an engraved cigarette case, and extracted from it a cigarette. He snapped shut the case. The click was mechanically perfect and snapped across the room. The Colonel gazed levelly at Flanck as he tapped the cigarette against the case. He considered his words carefully.

"I do not believe in nonsense, Herr Flanck. I believe it is now—four o'clock and the year is 1973. I believe at this moment, a man is roaming our streets with a cleaver eliminating people who resemble Nazis. The fact that he practices this liquidation twenty-eight years after the fact suggests that he is deranged. That is what I believe. I wish to discover more."

Colonel Schuckert flicked a mechanically perfect lighter. It burst into flame at once, a tall blue flame high over the gold. He lit his cigarette and blew the smoke out through his nostrils. He turned to Bauer.

"Continue, Inspector," Colonel Schuckert said.

Flanck's smile increased and he restrained himself, leaning against the dull black leather and studs of his chair.

Inspector Bauer licked his lips, and with a look at Colonel Schuckert continued. He tossed a photograph of the Auschwitz siding onto the table. Then he turned to Flanck.

"It is possible that persons who staffed the Birkenau death camp at Auschwitz are on his list of victims." Bauer turned to Madeline, who sat dispassionately at the far end of the conference table, alert, yet removed from the tensions among the Germans. "Miss Kress," Bauer said.

Madeline opened a large manila envelope and took out a sheaf of photographs. These, too, she slowly passed to Colonel Schuckert, one by one as she spoke, and Schuckert at length turned them over to the inspectors across the table.

"These are the pictures of the staff in charge of the camp at Auschwitz," she said.

A photograph made its way into the Inspector's hands.

"Dr. Mengele—in charge of the internees."

Other photographs entered Colonel Schuckert's large hands. "His aides—Dr. Rhode—"

The photographs were passed down the long table to Flanck.

95

"Doctors Tilot, Klein, and Muller."

The photographs piled in front of Flanck's drumming fingers. He continued to look narrowly at the young Israeli woman.

"His helpers—Tauber, Kramer, Emmerich, Froelich."

Madeline pulled out the photographs from the sheaf in her lap.

"Leader of the Women's Camp—Frau Mandel."

The German policemen gazed down at the faces, grainy and resurrected from the past. On each, a different expression fleetingly crossed the lips and eyes. Bauer stared hard at the primitive, sadistic faces of the Third Reich. Flanck continued to ignore the photographs, impatiently waiting.

"There are others—Stiblitz, Perschel, Honig, and an assortment of functionaries. But I don't have the pictures."

Madeline leaned back softly. District Attorney Flanck looked hard at her and then turned to Bauer.

"Very educational, Bauer," he said. "How does it help you to catch a killer?"

"I think we should run these photographs in the Munich newspapers."

Flanck's smile deepened.

"You're joking," he said.

"There are people in this city who resemble the people in these photographs. The killer will be looking for them. We can find them first, and set them as decoys."

Flanck looked around the room to see the reactions on the other faces. They were neutral, and so he returned to Bauer.

"You mean just . . . hand them out to the newspapers?"

Bauer licked his lips and passed his fingertips across his forehead.

"I see no alternative," Bauer said. "Unless you're willing to assume the responsibility for any future murders."

Flanck rose and moved slowly to Bauer's side of the table. All eyes were upon him.

"No, Inspector. For the time being, the responsibility is all yours." Flanck studied his words, rolling them in his thin lips before speaking. "I might add, however, that if your best suggestion is a parade of these crackpot theories across the front pages of our newspapers, I think you should be removed from the case."

Colonel Schuckert sighed.

"That would be my decision to make, Herr Flanck," Colonel Schuckert said.

Flanck's lethal smile poured across the table at the Colonel.

"You're quite right, Colonel." He paced the floor quietly, on his soft rubber-soled shoes. "You're quite right. It is, in fact, four o'clock in the afternoon. Twenty-eight years have passed. The Nazis are dead. For twenty-eight years Germany has paid for their crimes. . . ." Flanck eyed Bauer. ". . . And paid . . . and paid." Flanck paused directly behind Bauer. The smile left his face. "My God, Bauer," he continued hoarsely, and with a note of appeal, "we've barely shut the door on the Olympic tragedy, and here you are suggesting we spread a full-scale revival of the past across the newspapers of the world. Have you lost your senses? Do you realize the implications of what you propose?"

Colonel Schuckert's face narrowed as he rigidly watched the small District Attorney.

"All right, Flanck," Colonel Schuckert said. "For now we will forget the newspapers." The Colonel turned briskly to Bauer. "Let's get on with this, Bauer. What, in a practical sense, is being done?"

"We're checking every mental institution in Germany. There are over five hundred. Prisons, political files, war hospitals are being checked. The only true lead is this picture of Auschwitz junction. It is quite possible the killer spent time in Auschwitz during the war. If there are good records of the inmates, we may identify him eventually."

From the end of the conference table came Madeline's voice. "They destroyed the records."

The men stared at her. Her face was illumined by a strange smile, both confident and hateful.

"They burned them with the bodies," she said.

Flanck leaned over the edge of the table.

"Can we trust her?" he asked.

Bauer rose in anger. His chair fell over backward. Colonel Schuckert rose equally quickly and put a restraining arm on Bauer's shoulder.

"I am responsible for Miss Kress, Herr Flanck," Colonel Schuckert said.

He moved around Bauer, smiling, and walked toward Madeline. With a kind of old Prussian charm, he spoke, loudly enough for all the men to hear.

"Thank you so much, my dear," he said, "for all your help. And now I'm sure you must be famished." He turned slightly to Bauer, who still stared angrily at Flanck.

"Eh, Bauer . . ."

Bauer tore his eyes from Flanck and turned to Schuckert and Madeline.

"Sir?"

"Miss Kress is hungry," Colonel Schuckert said. "If you don't do something about it, I certainly shall."

Bauer approached the chair on which Madeline sat. His face softened.

"I'll take care of it, sir," he said.

"Herr Flanck," Colonel Schuckert said. "We will confer again when the case has developed."

"Colonel Schuckert," Flanck said, with a turn of his head that passed for a bow.

The policemen of Munich left the room, Colonel Schuckert ushering Madeline through the black paneled doors. Flanck followed their departure in restrained silence. When the departing footsteps had died away down the halls, he reached out onto the table and angrily pushed the photographs away from him. Ernst Kaltenbrunner and thirty-three Jews in winter overcoats standing at a train siding in Auschwitz fell off the far end of the long conference table, and revolved downward into the shadow, and onto the floor.

*　　*　　*

"Oh, my God!" the woman whispered.

The group huddled in the darkness held its breath. Smoke from cigarettes ascended to the ceiling. Silence reigned. Then, up front, the acrobat, balanced on a chair, which teeteringly balanced on a ball, which in turn rolled slowly over a table, raised one arm, leaving herself balanced on the other.

The audience, as one, exhaled and applauded. Then the band struck up its melody and the acrobat, a thin young woman with small breasts, in a white lamé suit, leaped down off the chair and caught up the ball in her arms. With copious bows, she made her way to the waiting wings while the audience roared and thundered its approval. The tumult died away, and there was the talking and the clinking of wineglasses.

Martin Bauer poured wine into Madeline's glass. They sat in the mezzanine, overlooking the stage, with a kind of red plush curtain at their backs. Bauer thought he had seen a glimmer of enjoyment in the Israeli's eyes, but when she turned back, after the lights were on, she was as hard and steady as ever.

"You've changed your hair style," he said. "It becomes you. Not so severe."

The woman fascinated Bauer. There was something so German about her, and yet so totally alien.

"Do you dance, Miss Kress?"

"I think we should understand each other, Inspector. I am here to help catch your killer. Nothing else."

Bauer reddened somewhat. The band caught on to a livelier tune, and he watched the younger couples step onto the dancing floor. At length the dance stopped and the music trailed into an improvisation.

Bauer turned toward Madeline again.

"Let me ask you this, then, Miss Kress. You know Munich, don't you?"

"I was born here."

"Where?"

"By the Old South Cemetery."

"By the river?" he asked.

"By the Wittelsbach bridge."

Bauer nodded.

"You must have . . . feelings being back here."

". . . None."

"None?"

She shrugged, yet not entirely with indifference.

"I died here, Inspector. It means nothing to me now."

Bauer's eyes lowered. He said gently, "I think I understand."

"I doubt it, Inspector. You cannot."

Martin Bauer's reply was drowned out in the rising tide of applause from the audience. The lights dimmed. They were in total darkness for a moment, and then a spotlight caught the stunning figure of a woman, seemingly poured into a clinging, sequined gown, standing starkly at the microphone. A hush fell over the room as the band tapped out a languorous introduction, and the woman began to sing.

> *"Oktoberfest—*
> *Oktoberfest—*
> *When hearts convene—*
> *To play a scene—*
> *A masquerade—*
> *A sad charade—*
> *October's jest—*
> *Oktoberfest—"*

Bauer noticed that Madeline watched nothing, nor did she seem to be listening. Several people in the audience began to join in the singing.

> "November sings—
> December cheers—
> September brings—
> October tears—
> October sighs—
> October lies—
> Oktoberfest—
> Oktoberfest—"

Bauer's eyes traversed the room, moving from the singer, caught and held in the white circle of light, past the rows of patrons, listening wistfully to the strong heady voice, and finally coming to rest on Madeline's clear, gray eyes, staring hard and unblinking at her untouched wine. Was it his imagination, or was that sadness, even loneliness, he saw just beneath that carefully composed veneer of anger and hostility? Bauer suddenly felt strangely touched.

"Suffering . . . has been universal," he said, leaning forward. "I think you will find a great sympathy in Germany today for the victims of the past."

"Like Flanck? Is he sympathetic?"

"I am sorry about Flanck. But he is only ambitious. It has nothing to do with you."

"That's hard to believe."

"Don't you see?" Bauer looked down, thinking for his words. "In the last war, there were only victims. Perhaps now, finally, there is the time for—"

"Forgiveness?"

Bauer looked up.

"If not forgiveness—then understanding."

"There are a thousand German tourists in Israel every year,

and they all want the same thing." Madeline looked at him with her hard, brilliant eyes. "Well—I cannot give it to them. And I cannot give it to you, Inspector. I don't care to hear about your little guilts."

A tone of red crept into the Inspector's face. He said nothing. All around them a hundred voices joined the singer in a reprise of the final chorus.

> *"So let us live—*
> *For passion's sake—*
> *What summers give—*
> *Octobers take—*
> *So live for cheer—*
> *For love and beer—*
> *Forget the rest—*
> *Oktoberfest—"*

The song ended in a whisper. The approval of the audience approached an ovation, and as the singer bowed her way to the wings, the band took up where it had left off, with soft American jazz. Throughout it all, Madeline's eyes remained fixed on the Inspector's face.

"How did you think I knew about Kaltenbrunner? And Klein? And Tauber?" Madeline continued as the tumult began to lessen. "I went to a hard school to learn about them. I could not forget them if I wanted to. They killed my mother, and my father, and my brothers, and all my people. And they were polite, inquisitive, obedient, normal Germans such as yourself!"

Bauer paled.

"What's wrong, Inspector? Do you deny it?"

"No," he said softly, "not that."

Madeline followed his gaze down to the table. There her wrist lay exposed from the tweed coat. She removed her hand from the table, and the blue tattooed number disappeared again under her coat sleeve.

The Inspector remained silent for some time. Finally he leaned forward, though not yet confronting the hard gray eyes.

"What you say is true," he said, "but we are still living. You are an attractive woman, yet you spend your days in a mausoleum, surrounded by corpses—"

"Not corpses, Inspector," Madeline said in almost a whisper. "My people."

Before Bauer could help her, Madeline rose and threw on her coat. The two of them made their way through the milling crowd at the entrance, and out onto the brightly lit streets once again.

At Wittelsbach fountain, a chain of firecrackers exploded in their midst, taking Madeline completely by surprise. She leaned against the Inspector for support, though it troubled her that he touched her. Bauer guided her through the milling crowd and into his blue Mercedes.

They drove together in silence over the Isar River. Bauer drove out a bit into the countryside, to cool Madeline's nerves, and then back toward the city. The wind blew lightly through the tall grasses. Bullfrogs creaked from somewhere in the hidden ponds. They drove back over the Isar River, and the water was black, rippling, splashing down through the water grasses.

"Miss Kress," he said.

He turned and saw, as the car went smoothly in and out of the moonlight, under the trees, that she was asleep. Her long brown hair fell out upon the back of the seat, and the slender face seemed calm now, for the first time. From time to time he looked at her, as he drove her home.

"Miss Kress."

Startled, she awoke.

"We are home," he said.

They walked out into the crisp autumn air, through the crisp leaves gathered over the lawn, over the dark oak roots that buckled up out of the earth. They walked to the door of Bauer's apartment house.

Frank De Felitta

"Good night, Inspector," Madeline said. "Thank you for dinner."

"Good night, Miss Kress."

The Inspector bowed politely and left for his car.

Madeline closed the outer door and the inner door. Inside, she opened all shutters, as if there was never enough air in the German's apartment. Her feet creaked on the tile floor.

She took a teakettle from the shelf and, while the room was still dark, she filled the kettle with water and put it on the stove burner. She took a cup from the shelf, and a saucer. She sat down in the darkness of the kitchen, beside the lacy white curtains which blew in the breeze, and she tried to understand why she had come back.

Germany seems so peaceful, Madeline thought.

It was always peaceful. The Wittelsbach bridge. The old synagogue. Markets and flowers. Until the marching. Then it began. A progression of pictures flashing through her mind, faster and faster, beyond her control—of the burnings, the staging areas in Munich, the freight cars, the dyings, and the daily killings—

The teakettle screamed.

Madeline, perspiring, suddenly feeling faint, turned off the gas jet and tried to control her thoughts more carefully. Nervously, trembling with an inner cold, she sat in the dark, alone. She still could not understand why she had come back.

CHAPTER NINE

The night wore on. Munich celebrated its ordeal. No one slept. Its millions swarmed through the streets, dancing, carousing, and drinking, scattered now through the old town and the fairgrounds. Parties were formed on the meadows outside of town, as far as Schleissheim and Dachau, the little villages lighted late at night.

Only the neighborhood of the construction site seemed strangely untouched by the gaiety. The raucous sounds of celebration were here only a distant noise.

Within the cramped shelter of the gutted building, the man sat immobile with fear, scarcely drawing breath. A ball, a child's ball, had somehow found its way through a narrow crevice at the base of the destroyed wall, and rolled to a stop against his left shoe. Outside the shelter, unseen, two people were engaged in a taut dialogue.

"What are you up to?" said the strong, male voice.

"My ball," said a young boy's voice. "It went in there."

"It's after ten o'clock. What are you doing on the street so late?"

"Just playing."

"Playing? At this time of night?"

"My mother and father are at the pavilions."

"I see," said the strong voice, with a tinge of humor. "And while the cats are away, the little mouse decided to have a bit of fun. All right, watch out . . . let me have a look."

The heavy crunch of rocks and earth outside the shelter signaled the approach of footsteps. Amidst grunts and groans, a shadowy figure slowly descended to the level of the opening.

Silently, the man's hand reached forth and gave the ball a gentle push toward the opening; but a jutting stone deviated its forward momentum and caused it to arc in a curve toward a deeper recess of the shelter. Before the man could move to remedy the situation, the harsh glare of an electric torch thrust itself through the opening, sending exploring beams dancing about the narrow enclosure. The man pressed his back hard against the brick wall and he stopped drawing breath. Twice, the ferreting beam skittered across the dusty sole of his left shoe, but thankfully did not pause. At last, the light fell upon the ball and held it in its grasp.

"I see it," said the strong voice.

Suddenly, as if propelled by its own volition, the electric torch snaked through the crevice and entered the shelter. Attached to it were a hand and a blue sleeve, brandishing the gold braid and brass of authority.

The man continued to hold his breath tightly, as the torch prodded and poked at the ball, encouraging it forward toward the opening. Once, the hand holding the torch actually brushed against the man's shoe, sending a shock of animal fear coursing through his tense body. But still he managed to maintain the posture of total rigidity, his fever-bright eyes bulging under the strain of the ordeal. At last, the torch and the ball were with-drawn from the shelter.

"Here, now," said the strong voice, panting slightly. "Go to your home, and hurry!"

"Thank you," said the young boy's voice.

The sounds of footsteps leaving—the lighter footsteps run-ning, the heavier footsteps trudging slowly—gradually faded and merged with the distant noises from the pavilions. Only then did the man allow himself the luxury of relieving his bursting lungs.

For some minutes thereafter, the only sounds to be heard in the vicinity of the construction site were terrible, racking coughs and gasps, followed by another, gentler sound: the sound of a man weeping.

*   *   *

In the Justice Building, Inspector Steinman stood in front of Koenig. At Steinman's elbow was the coffeepot from the front hall switchboard.

"Tell me again what happened," Steinman said.

"I asked the American commander if there were any unau-thorized absences on the first, second, and sixth days of the Ok-toberfest specifically, or during that week generally—"

"But you didn't see the rolls yourself."

"No, sir."

Steinman wearily drained the last of the coffee from the steel percolator. He looked at the dregs in the cup, raised it to his lips, grimaced, and then put it back on the table. In the distant hall-way, two uniformed policemen brought in a young man with greased hair combed backward, fighting drunk.

"Now listen, Koenig," Steinman said. "You made a mistake. You don't know the commander. You don't know what kind of man he is. Maybe he was embarrassed by your saying, 'unau-thorized absences.' You can't know." Steinman paused. "And you can't be intimidated. It was your duty to see the rolls."

"Sir, I had no authority."

"Then you should have returned here and received it."

A woman, dressed in costume, came into the outer hall, weeping hysterically. Steinman motioned to the uniformed desk clerk, who rose with a sigh and slowly approached the swaying woman.

"Now look at the Chief Inspector," Steinman said, turning back to Koenig. "How did he get to be Chief Inspector? Because he is relentless. He is never intimidated."

Steinman raised a finger.

"He went to Paris and the Middle East at great personal expense. And risk, Koenig, risk, for a case which perplexed him."

"Yes, sir."

Steinman decided to drink the coffee after all. He closed his eyes and lifted the cup. It was a quick, unpleasant drink.

"Take him as an example, Koenig, the next time you go out into the field. Or you will be the oldest patrolman in the history of the Munich Police."

"Yes, sir."

Steinman waved a hand, indicating that Koenig should leave. Koenig snapped his heels and walked down the hall with new energy. Steinman watched him go and shook his head.

Steinman looked at his watch. The hour was nearly up. There would still be time to get to the fairgrounds and, if he drank quickly enough, time to catch up. He reached into the switchboard for the telephone and called Marlene.

Steinman drove out in his new car, brightly under the festival lights, for Marlene's apartment. The crowds were in front and in back of his car. Everywhere the flesh tones flickered under the dancing lights.

*   *   *

Hugo Flanck banged down the telephone receiver. Quickly, he snatched it up again.

"No, no. I must speak with him personally."

Impatiently, he strained to hear the voice of the long-distance operator. In the adjoining room, the Oktoberfest was going full blast. Women shrieked with laughter, and the foul American rock music, which seemed to have infected the whole of Munich, blared out its brassy noise. Flanck pounded on the wall with the flat of his hand, but to no avail.

"District Attorney Flanck!" he yelled back to the operator.

He drummed his fingers on the table top. His long, thin fingers quickly shuffled the papers on his table and set them into rows, then reset them again. Suddenly the fingers stopped and he smiled.

"Good evening, sir," he said suavely. "I know it is late but the line . . . Yes, from Munich. . . . I hope you were not sleeping . . ." Flanck held the receiver in both hands. "Yes . . . a series of strange murders here . . . Perhaps the news has reached the North? . . . A strange relation . . ." Flanck continued, enunciating clearly into the black telephone. "Not only as District Attorney, but as your personal friend and member of the Coalition, I felt it my duty to speak with you directly. . . ."

When he was through and had hung up, the smile faded very, very slowly, as though it hung there separately, in the room, and, as other thoughts crossed Flanck's mind, it distorted utterly, until there was no recognizable expression at all.

Had the conversation gone well? Yes, it had gone well. He had done a personal favor in alerting the Ministry. It could only go well from now on.

Flanck breathed generously the cold air coming in from the hills. Now the noise of the Oktoberfest seemed more musical to his ears. For a fleeting moment, Flanck considered throwing himself into the party next door, but restrained himself. Instead, still filled with excitement, he looked out the window. The stars shone over the meadows, clear and endless, and seemed to be conveying to him secret messages of power he, as yet, could only sense. Flanck's ambitions had scope.

And he was proud to be a German. Proud to be one of the strong, indefatigable German people.

*   *   *

"Was there anything else you wanted, my dear?"

There was no answer.

The woman, wearing a white negligee, carried on a small silver tray a crystal glass and a decanter of amber brandy. She set the tray on the lamp table nearest her husband. After twenty-two years of marriage, she knew when he wanted to be left alone.

Colonel Schuckert put aside his cigar. He reached for the glass of brandy and drank it slowly. He returned it a moment later, empty.

The neon lights of Munich colored the textiles of the room's draperies a subtle red. Silent sparks rose up from the intersections where blue streetcars turned the corners. Karl's Gate flickered in the holiday lights.

Normally, Colonel Schuckert enjoyed looking down into the changing night colors, the faces of young men and women dodging the traffic, laughing in the excitement of youth, and the Oktoberfest itself. But the cleaver killer had attacked the Colonel as surely as he had sliced into his victims, and now the tumult filled him instead with a great sense of sorrow.

For Schuckert remembered. After four hours in the room with the young Israeli woman, Schuckert could not help but remember.

These squares and alleys, filled with the brown shirts and the black, with hypnotized young men, nightly murders and beatings, while the Army stood aloof. It was out of control. None could stop it, once it started—the insanity of the Austrian corporal.

Colonel Schuckert held the brandy glass to his lips, but it was empty. —But that Germany, itself, should have lost its mind . . .

"It's getting late, my dear," came the soft voice from the end of the room.

Colonel Schuckert turned. Silhouetted against the hallway chandelier was the form of the woman he trusted more than any man or institution in the world. She waited for him.

"A small brandy, if you would," Colonel Schuckert said softly.

He turned his head and heard the sound of the crystal decanter against another crystal glass.

"Thank you, my dear," Colonel Schuckert said.

"Maniac!" screamed a woman.

Below, a driver swerved in and out of the light, scattering pedestrians down the avenue. Colonel Schuckert leaned out of the window.

In these streets, Colonel Schuckert had led his patrols in search of looters after the war. That was when the Germans had screamed for the Cyklon B gas. Highly indignant. That it should go to the Jews. When the bombs were falling day by day. Misuse. Madness.

"Why, Heinrich," she said, approaching from the shadows. "Your eyes—there are tears in them."

"Too much brandy," the Colonel said. "The eyes, you know . . ." He smiled.

Schuckert looked down sadly on the faces of hurrying people, running among the crossroads, cars blowing their horns and shouting voices.

". . . The eyes see too much," the Colonel said.

*   *   *

Five murders so far, three of which involved a butcher's cleaver and the mutilation of the bodies. Seven beatings, two

attempted suicides. Vandalism too prevalent to have been item-
ized yet. A number of foreigners were missing their wives. The
police were overwhelmed. And still, this was the greatest Oktoberfest since the war. The breweries had seen nothing like it.
Three million liters of double-strength brew had been drunk so
far, and the festival was only half over. Five tons of fresh-water
fish, roasted live over long mounds of white-hot coals on the
ground, glowing and crackling far into the night. Oxen, spitted
whole, revolved slowly over the open hearths. Pork—enough to
link itself around the entire city limits. There was no end to it.
And the foreign currency was pouring in like water.

"Come on!" Steinman called to Marlene's upstairs window.
"We'll be late!"

Marlene hurried down the stairs, wearing a short white coat,
her hair curled at the ears, forward. She got into the car, and
Steinman drove crazily toward the fairgrounds.

They parked and then began to edge their way into the crowd
of the pavilion. Marlene held onto Steinman's hand, and they
merged in the heat of the crowd and fought for space to dance.
The roar was intolerable, the band on its podium pounded and
blared over their ears, the steins banged, and the students and
sailors, nearly insensate from beer, turned and whirled in a puls-
ing, bleary vision. Steinman and Marlene danced and danced,
their bodies exhausted and hot, lost in the continuous delirium
that was the Oktoberfest.

They were in the largest beer hall in the world. The blue and
yellow streamers seemed to come down from the heavens, and
the band, its tinny brass and drums thumping in an acre of
Germans, carried Steinman, like a cork on a wave, in its thrust.

Steinman was becoming drunk. He drank and drank until the
crowd turned into disembodied faces which floated in strange
color tones around his eyes. He drank from the steins, among
the Vikings, the Bears, the Clowns, the Bavarians and their
Kings and Princes, until the heat of the crowd washed over him

and drowned him and he sat down suddenly on a chair, not having remembered that at all, and laughed.

He left the table laughing, and made his way, past Marlene, toward the door. At the entrance, an old man fell upon him, embraced him, and indicated that they sit down together and have a stein of beer. Steinman laughed and pushed the old man gently into the crowd. Steinman walked out into the night, black and cold and clear as the original universe.

There, under the stars, he staggered down through the grass left alive on the midway, laughing to himself, smelling the cold autumn breeze coming in from the surrounding hayfields.

Far away, in front of him, illuminated from below, were the tents of the "beer corpses." Men and women who drank until they could no longer remember their names, let alone how to get home, and so they slept the night there. Steinman laughed; he was not yet a "corpse." He leaned against a telephone pole.

The crowds flowed and melded colorfully, violently among each other. Away from them now, Steinman looked back on the seven pavilions stretched out on the edge of the meadows. From each came a roar—the roar of banging steins and drinking songs and boots on the wooden tables. And adulteries and fist fights. Mindlessly packed together. The roar of the great German festival.

Steinman closed his eyes, and became ill against the shadow of the telephone pole, as a distant church bell tolled the hour of midnight.

MUNICH:
The Tenth Day of Oktoberfest

CHAPTER TEN

Hilda Dorn came tipsily out of the beer hall. A young woman, about twenty-four, with blond hair, dyed, and a black dress with loose straps, she was pretty. She stumbled out along the sidewalk. Inside, the men sat stiffly, woodenly, drinking themselves drunk. Nevertheless, it had been a fair night for her. She had money in her purse. A raucous accordion blared out of the beer hall.

The moon was not visible; a silvery luminescence slid underneath a stream of clouds. Autumn leaves had collected at the bottom of the black iron railings, and the breeze which blew came straight from the meadows, carrying coolness and the smell of pollen in the air.

In the shadows of an alley, a man watched her.

"Come on," she said, winking her left eye. "Don't be shy."

Old arches bent over the cobblestone streets. Birds, black in
the night, had roosted among the porticoes, and from their dark-
beaked forms, circling and resting, came the hooting, mournful
cries. Rococo, brought to Germany by Ludwig the First from
Italy, graced the night in long twisted columns, the tiny figures
turning among each other in stone. Hilda walked down the old
alleys, her red shoes shining.

Her hips swayed methodically. She hiccuped. The sounds
echoed. She laughed. How absurd, to hiccup among such pon-
derous stone. She belched softly.

"Du, du, liegst mir im Herzen," she taunted.

She looked behind her. Hesitantly, irregularly, the man continued to stalk her.

Down the long alley, a single light bulb, shielded in a metal
guard, hung from wires strung across the brick and stone walls.
It illuminated nothing below. The windows above reflected a
vastly distant luminescent cloud, as though eyes on the brick
walls, one by one, watched her go by.

The man came up the long alley after Hilda.

In a long dingy building, replastered so many times that the
front resembled more a wall from one end to the other than a
series of close-neighboring, narrow houses, a number of heavy,
splintered wooden doors stood in a row.

Hilda affected a stone in her shoe. She leaned over to dislodge
it. A generous amount of leg was revealed under the lacy black
dress. No petticoat. Young legs, firm and thin. Hilda stood upright and fumbled for the keys to the door at which she had
stopped.

The knotholes, like eyes, stared at her. She pulled for the key
on a ring and inserted it into the lock. Then she entered a long,
dingy, unlit hallway. Bits of plaster, having been swept from
the floor, lay alongside the baseboard of the walls. Stairs led to
nowhere that one could see. A dark well swallowed them.
Chandeliers which had no lights and were made of cheap glass

followed her progress underneath. She fumbled for the key ring and pulled on a second key, aware of the man's footsteps approaching outside.

The man would try the door, she hoped.

Hilda inserted the second key and opened the door to her room. She entered and closed the door behind her. She listened. But the man did not enter the corridor.

"*Scheiss*," she said. The men don't come any more. It is the Oktoberfest. The beer. Hilda would have to go to the fairgrounds or call it a night.

Hilda's room was simple, unadorned. On a bureau, a small icon of the Virgin leaned against a mirror. A stuffed bear, wearing the label of a brewery, leaned against the other side of the mirror.

Hilda pursed her lips and began to fix her make-up. Lipstick, applied with care, rounded her mouth and made it glisten. It encased the lips in deep color. Black from the eyes had smudged; she restored it with a black pencil. The lashes stood out, startlingly upright and dark, from her face. And the cheeks she made red with a density that made her face into a mask. Hilda admired her hair; it was still her pride. Light, though thinned by dyes, it looped gently over her forehead. Her face was a clear sign to men of who she was, and what she wanted.

Hilda listened. Outside, in the other side of the building, beyond her window, men were talking, low and coarse, and passing by, leaving drifts of conversations with unmistakable intentions as they assessed and evaluated the comparative merits of each girl behind her respective window.

Hilda undressed, wearily and by rote.

In her black panties and black, low-cut brassiere, she sat in an overstuffed chair beside the venetian blinds at the window. She drank beer from a glass she had obtained from the kitchen pantry beyond the large white bed. The bed dominated the room.

The voices had stilled outside. A lonely night. Hilda drank. Where were her cigarettes? Hilda drank.

She sighed.

She leaned back somewhat, and in a routine gesture, she reached out and partially opened the blind.

"Oh!"

Dark, dark eyes stared in at her.

The venetian blinds cut a black grid of shadow across the heavy face. His eyes were black, and filled with a hatred Hilda had never before seen.

An enormous blade smashed the window. Bits of glass flew inward, showering Hilda Dorn. She screamed. She threw her arms in front of her.

The blade smashed its way into the interior, and the eyes appeared, concentrated upon her, and then the arm followed, grabbing for a hold.

Hilda pulled her robe from a hook on the door and ran.

Hysterically, she ran up the stairs, into the pitch-black stairwell. Cobwebs brushed against her face. Things scattered from under her feet. Thrashing furniture sounded below her.

The man came through the open door, into the corridor.

Hilda ran upstairs, her bare feet tripping over the crumbled stone steps. She threw herself through an open doorway, and then out onto the roof. She stepped among broken glass. The cold air cut through her flimsy underclothes. Her teeth chattered. The man was no longer making noise below. Where had he gone? Hilda trembled until she became frigid with fear, not knowing whether to stay on the roof, lest he be coming quietly up the stairs, or to climb down the fire escape, lest he be down there, waiting, among the shadows of the alley. Crying, whimpering uncontrollably, Hilda climbed down the fire escape and ran along the streets babbling, until three citizens and, finally, the police stopped her.

*   *   *

"Eyes!" Hilda said. "Huge, terrible eyes—!"

Bauer and Steinman stood over Hilda at the desk in the first interrogation room. The light bulb in its shield hung directly over her, and glared down over the face streaked with trails of mascara intermixed with rouge. Hilda trembled uncontrollably.

Steinman held out a cup of hot chocolate. The steam twirled uselessly into the light. She seemed not to see the men.

At the far cabinet, Colonel Schuckert stood immobile, his arms folded, watching the young prostitute. His own eyes were red, and a tic had formed at the side of his mouth. He seemed to be in continual conversation with himself. He mumbled from time to time, considered, and then became silent.

Bauer and Steinman exchanged glances. It was past three in the morning, and neither had slept since the night before.

Colonel Schuckert roamed around the room, his eye taken by various objects on the wall and, finally, taken again by the sight of Hilda Dorn.

"She saw him?" the Colonel said.

Bauer shrugged with an infinitely small gesture.

"Someone smashed her window with what appeared to have been a butcher's cleaver and kept on coming for her," Bauer said.

"He came in so fast," Hilda wailed. "Like an animal!"

Colonel Schuckert brushed his hair back with his hands. He straightened the edge of his coat. It seemed to make him feel better. Nervously, he crooked his neck. The uniform had not been cleaned the previous night.

"But the description," Colonel Schuckert said, "the man. Who was he?"

"Not yet, sir," Bauer said. "She can't calm down."

Steinman drank the chocolate, as it had gone cold. He shrugged, and left for another cup.

"In her profession, it could have been a disgruntled client," Colonel Schuckert said.

"Very disgruntled, sir," Bauer said.

Out of the shadow, an eye moved. Flanck, having sat immobile, could restrain himself no longer.

"Certainly not," Flanck said. "This young lady is well known. It was obviously the anti-Nazi underground which sent out orders to have her liquidated."

"I didn't say that, sir," Bauer said.

Flanck rose from his chair under the window. He wore a gray double-breasted coat, which served him as a raincoat. Stiffly, the fabric creaked as he approached the center of the room.

"Don't be too sure, Bauer," Flanck said, as he reached down and jerked up Hilda's head from her arms. He held it there, her chin in the palm of his hand. "Tell me, does she resemble Adolf Hitler? Rudolf Hess? A little sweep of the comb and—look, it's Goebbels!" He let go of her face. His voice rose slightly. "What in the name of the Federal Republic is going on here? Are you insane? Someone wants to get to a whore, and you have her history examined! You call in the Colonel himself, and—"

"Excuse me, sir," Bauer said in a strained but quiet voice. "I am trying to find a man who has killed three people. He perhaps has threatened a fourth. I intend to use her to capture him. If you have some other program for stopping him, please, sir, proceed."

Flanck stood now directly opposite Bauer. The intensity in their eyes were a direct match for each other.

"Look, Bauer," Flanck said. "You're a simpleton. If you continue with this irrational line of reasoning, we won't be able to keep this quiet. It can't be done. And then what will happen? The foreign press will eat this like honey cake, distort it—" Flanck addressed Bauer with the patience one would a child who is having trouble with a basic principle. "There are times when the press can be your enemy, Bauer. You must develop a sensitivity to these things," Flanck concluded.

"The District Attorney's sensitivities are well known," Bauer said, lighting a cigarette slowly in Flanck's face. "As for me—the case is very important." Bauer looked directly at Flanck. "And I will solve it."

Flanck smiled. He raised an eyebrow. He put forth a finger in a warning gesture and, in a soft voice, almost kindly, he whispered, "Be careful, Bauer."

Steinman came in through the door, holding a paper cup of steaming chocolate. He looked from Bauer to Flanck, and tip-toed to the center of the room. Hilda gently sobbed.

The tension, however, was broken.

Flanck sat down abruptly on a chair opposite Hilda Dorn. His fingers drummed impatiently on the table.

"Well—" Flanck began, "proceed, Bauer."

"We have a little wait," Bauer said.

"For whom?"

"Kress."

The men, perspiring in the hot and humid night air, waited with weary, sleep-ridden eyes. The clock moved slowly; it hummed, over their heads. Hilda fell into a light, uneasy sleep. Steinman let her. Again the cup of chocolate went cold. Steinman, his coat off, sat slumped in a chair. Colonel Schuckert retired to his post beside the metal filing cabinets. Bauer was running out of cigarettes.

In fifteen more minutes, the door opened. Madeline Kress walked in. She, too, had not slept that night. Her face, however, was both curious and alert.

The men stirred. Bauer joined her at the door.

"Thank you for coming," he said.

He took her by the elbow and led her around the front desk. Flanck rather stiffly let her pass. Bauer and Madeline stood over Hilda Dorn.

"A prostitute," Bauer said quietly. "Her name is Hilda Dorn. No history of her, yet. But she may have seen the killer to-night."

Madeline stood over the young girl. Hilda sensed someone

watching her and, with a start, looked up. She saw Madeline's clear gray eyes looking down on her. Hilda turned away from Madeline and looked from man to man, her face streaked with the paths of tears through the make-up.

"Who's she?" Hilda asked.

But no one said a word.

"What does she want?" Hilda demanded, her voice rising. The men only stared at her.

Madeline reached down with a white handkerchief in her hand, and touched Hilda on the cheek. Hilda, startled, withdrew. But Madeline reached down still farther and wiped the black trails from Hilda's cheeks.

Hilda smiled hesitantly.

Madeline looked at Hilda carefully. Turning the handkerchief over, she used the clean side, and continued to remove the black and the red until, finally, the skin tones showed through under the brimming eyes.

Madeline's eyes narrowed. With great distaste, she let go of the girl's head.

"What is it?" Bauer asked.

Madeline, backing away, looked at Hilda with growing fear and horror mingled with intense hatred.

"What's wrong?" Hilda moaned. "Why is she looking at me like that?"

Bauer and Steinman walked closer to Madeline, who stood rooted, staring not at Hilda Dorn, but at the nightmare specter from a past hell.

"Stop it!" Hilda screamed. She pointed at Madeline. "Make her stop it! That's the way *he* looked at me! Just like that—before he broke into my room!"

Madeline's lips moved. But no words came. She seemed to taste a bitter word. It fouled her lips.

"Bormann," Madeline whispered. "Juana Bormann."

Inspector Bauer whispered in Madeline's ear. "Auschwitz?"

Madeline nodded.

"She took care of the children."

"What's she talking about?" Hilda demanded.

"She put them in the lines," Madeline said. "And those who were not strong she strangled."

"I'm Hilda Dorn! Hilda Dorn! I never heard of Juana Bormann!"

Hilda looked around wildly. Steinman placed a restraining hand on her shoulder.

"Of course," Bauer said. He leaned over Hilda, speaking closely to her face. "Of course you're Hilda Dorn. You only look like Juana Bormann."

"But are you sure, Miss Kress?" Colonel Schuckert whispered hoarsely. "Are you absolutely certain?"

Madeline continued to stare at Hilda.

"She looks like Juana Bormann to me," Madeline said.

"And to someone else, too," Colonel Schuckert added.

In the silence that followed, Flanck seemed to shrink even deeper into the shadows. He did not know what to make of it. Everyone was mad. They believed it. They would pursue it. He must consider, and consider, and then decide what to do.

In the center of the room, Colonel Schuckert leaned forward over the table. He wanted to study the face more closely. A mute, trembling face, partially cleaned of black and red, looked back at him, the eyes afraid, not understanding what was happening to her.

"Bormann?" Colonel Schuckert said to himself. "Juana Bormann?"

CHAPTER ELEVEN

The Colonel looked up. Where was he? The lights shone into the night. The buildings, like awesome forms of sculpture, towered overhead. He became aware of the night streets, the lonely passers-by walking past the little shops. He moved slightly and was aware of his uniform. It restored him to his senses.

He was in the back seat of a police car. Bauer sat on one side of him. Madeline Kress sat on the other. In the front seat sat Steinman and Koenig. Parked under a gently waving linden tree, they all seemed to be waiting for something.

"You don't recognize where we are?" Colonel Schuckert said, turning to Madeline.

She looked at him, a little startled.

"Near here was the beer hall putsch," Colonel Schuckert said.

"We are a little south of that, sir," Bauer corrected respectfully.

"Yes."

Bauer's ears detected a new, strange note in the Colonel's voice.

"Yes, Bauer. I stand corrected."

Across the street from the police car was a small, low-ceilinged beer hall. Through the doors could be seen long wooden tables and men, some old and with canes laid across the benches, drinking beer slowly from steins. An accordion player sang out a sentimental song. It was evident from the girls who sat among the men that this was an old established place. The girls wore their hair short, curled at the sides, and all had profuse coatings of red and black over their faces. The policemen watched them from the car.

Behind an alley that led to the beer hall, another patrol car, like a black shark through dark waters, cruised slowly down the asphalt.

Steinman's radio crackled. He listened closely, then turned to Bauer.

"She's through the alley now," Steinman said. "She's passed Rhumfordstrasse and is turning down her street."

Bauer pulled a street map from the inside pocket of his coat. He opened it on his lap and took out a black fountain pen from his breast pocket.

"Instruct them not to close in, but to remain out of sight," Bauer said.

Steinman leaned toward the microphone and pressed a button.

"All units. All units. Keep to cover until ordered otherwise."

In the distance the cathedral clock struck the hour.

"Eleven o'clock," Madeline said.

"Well," Bauer said. "If he's going to come tonight, it may as well be now."

Steinman turned again from the radio.

"She's approaching her apartment," he said.

Bauer's black fountain pen traced a thick line over the alley side streets. "Another hundred meters," he estimated. He leaned back, waiting.

Colonel Schuckert straightened the gloves on his hands. They had become twisted as he wound his watch. His eyes no longer saw his surroundings, and he spoke aloud, but to no one in particular.

"We *could* have killed him," Colonel Schuckert said. "I, personally, had dozens of opportunities. We all knew what they were doing. We were well aware of . . . everything. I suppose we could have killed him."

A heavy silence filled the automobile. Madeline and Bauer stared at the Colonel. In the front seat, Steinman and Koenig had heard, but dared not turn around. Colonel Schuckert cleared his throat and looked straight ahead.

"Sir," Steinman said at last, to Bauer.

"Yes, Paul," Bauer said.

"She has entered her apartment."

Bauer sighed. "Right," he said. He capped the fountain pen. He relaxed somewhat. "There's not much else to do but stake out the apartment. Will that be correct, sir?"

The Colonel made no response.

"Sir?" Bauer repeated.

The Colonel returned a glassy stare.

"What is it, Bauer?"

"Hilda Dorn has entered her apartment safely. I suggest that there be a stakeout both inside and around her apartment."

The Colonel listened. But whatever was on his mind still dominated it.

"By all means, Bauer. By all means," Colonel Schuckert said vaguely.

Bauer opened the door beside him.

"Let's go, then," he said.

Rapidly, the group dispersed from the car and walked onto

the sidewalk. Bauer hesitated a moment, then turned to Steinman.

"Paul," he said. "Take Miss Kress home."

"May I stay here with you?"

Bauer turned toward her.

"You've done enough. It's better that you get your rest for
tomorrow."

"I . . . want to see him . . . if he comes."

Bauer caught the sight of Steinman watching him.

"It could be dangerous, Miss Kress. Or we may wait all night
for nothing."

"I am prepared," she said stubbornly. "I want to see him."

The Inspector realized he had the authority to send her home.
But he needed her willing co-operation. He nodded.

"Let's go quickly now."

They walked rapidly under the billowing leaves of the trees
which grew out of protected areas in the roadside. Sticks and
scattered stones littered the sidewalks. An occasional man passed,
drunk, weary, not noticing the police car parked under the
linden trees.

Bauer led them through a small garden, a back yard, and
pushed back the gate of a broken fence. He led them through
the alleys.

Colonel Schuckert, puffing, his face reddened, looked around
wildly at the gables and walls as they passed, as though the
weathered stone, the broken figurine had more meaning for him
than anyone else.

Bauer glanced back from time to time to watch his Commissioner's face.

The Inspector led them behind a leaning stone cottage,
sunken a meter into the ground, and then over a mound of earth
in a deserted lot. There, in front of them, was the wall of doors
and, at right angles to it, on the other side of the building, a
series of windows lit from the inside, yellow and red. Behind

127

the lace curtains in each, a woman sat in an overstuffed chair, and men passed in groups, hesitantly, in front of the windows, sometimes mounting the steps into the dark interior. Soft music played from a radio.

Bauer spoke softly.

"We'll go inside the building next to Hilda's. Up the stairs to the roof, and over the skylight. Then we can come down inside without using the doors. I don't want to frighten him away."

The Colonel approached Bauer, breathing hard, perspiring heavily.

"A good idea, Bauer."

Bauer took him by the elbow. Speaking to him quietly, so the others could not hear, he said, "Sir, we still have the stairs to climb and all night to wait. If I may say so, sir, the strain may not be good for you."

Colonel Schuckert looked at him suspiciously, considering Bauer's words.

At length, he said, "Yes. You're right."

The Colonel seemed to have regained some of his composure. His breathing had returned to normal. But his face still showed a terrible strain.

"It *has* been a bestial affair," the Colonel concluded.

Bauer gestured to Koenig.

"Take the Colonel to his private car, then join us on the roof."

Koenig saluted, and he followed the old man past the groups of men at the windows who turned to stare at the Army officer among them.

"We must be quick and quiet," Bauer said to Madeline and Steinman, as he led them across the road and into the dark, deserted building. Sticks and cobwebs littered the floor, made them think of rats. Plumbing hung out of the plaster where it had not been sealed with care. Steinman closed the door carefully behind them.

Up the stairs they quickly went. Around a central cavity, a circular stone stairwell wound its way up toward the skylights. Steinman, Bauer, and Madeline stepped lightly, running upward into the total darkness. Footsteps resounded in the empty mausoleum of the building. Deserted corridors and wasted offices disappeared behind them, bits of wiring sticking out from pipes. When they got to the top, they paused.

"Do you have your breath?" Bauer asked.

Madeline nodded.

The Inspector pushed open the top door, which led onto the roof. The stars were extraordinarily bright, notwithstanding a cloud which had drifted in front of the moon.

Gingerly, Bauer picked his way across the roof toward the next building. Bits of broken glass covered the shingles, and the leavings of squirrels or rats, plus bits of gnawed apple cores and straw. Carefully avoiding the chimneys that bent out at weird angles, they made their way down to the roof over Hilda's room. It was a tarred area, leading to a door perched against the rotted balcony.

Bauer surveyed the neighborhood. Down below, outside by the lights of the beer hall, a man leaned against the brick wall, ostensibly looking for girls. Bauer knew him to be a plain-clothes man. In the park, on the other side of the alley, a patrol car slowly cruised around the fountains. On the far side of the baroque roofs, the former residence of a prince, two more men stood—plain-clothes men. All the others were hidden from sight.

Steinman wedged open the door with a pocketknife. He jerked the door. It opened.

"All right, we are going inside now," Bauer said quietly. He held out his hand for Steinman's pocket radio. Steinman took it from his belt.

"All units. Remain at your posts. Act on your own initiative, but do not frighten him away."

Bauer clicked the transmitter button. Then he clicked it back on again, adding, "Your most important orders are these: He must be taken alive. I repeat: He must be taken alive."

Madeline followed Steinman into the dingy recesses on the upper floors of Hilda's building. Bauer followed behind, and closed the rickety door.

The darkness was total. By looking sideways, they managed to pick out the limits of the stairs. Here, too, there was a central cavity and a staircase, but there was no railing. They hugged the wall and felt their way downstairs. Slowly they descended. Bauer touched Steinman on the shoulder. He wanted the radio.

"Koenig?" Bauer whispered into the speaker. "Are you alive? Where are you?"

At length came the muffled response.

"I couldn't open the door to the first building," Koenig complained. "But I'll be up on the roof immediately."

"Be careful of the wires," Bauer said. "And Koenig, when you come down the stairs, position yourself on the landing of the first floor. Sit down in the corner so you can cover the two floors simultaneously."

"Yes, sir. I'll be right there, sir."

Bauer returned the radio.

Walking down the first-floor corridor, Bauer noticed that in addition to the back door and the large door in front, there was an archway over a window, capable of admitting a man. Without breaking stride, he pointed this out to Steinman. Steinman gestured that, since all doorways fed into the same corridor, it was useless to try to cover all three separately.

Bauer suddenly paused.

From the far recesses of an unseen part of the building, a creaking noise was heard. No one could tell where the sound was coming from. Steinman looked at Bauer. Bauer pointed to a door against the wall.

Steinman tapped lightly on the door, twice, and then once again, louder. There was no response. Again he tapped, twice softly and a third tap, louder. Again, no one came.

"Why doesn't she answer, Martin?" Steinman whispered.

Again, from some part of the building—the creaking—it seemed now to be over their heads—was getting louder.

The door in front of them finally opened a trembling crack.

A haggard face, stupefied in liquor, appeared. Hilda looked balefully back at them. Her face was tear-stained. The make-up was once again streaked down her face, cutting through the rouge like tracks of a sled.

Steinman pushed the door open. Bauer nudged Hilda aside, and Madeline entered. Bauer closed the door, but left the latch open.

"It's you—" Hilda croaked.

Steinman put his finger in front of his lips. He took her arm and led her to the chair which was still surrounded by shattered glass on the floor. Hilda looked around in consternation.

Bauer and Madeline moved to the back of the room, in the darkness of the curtains. Only a dull, reddish lamp illuminated the mirror over the blue and white Virgin.

"Why did you bring her?" Hilda complained. "She's the one who said I killed babies."

"Shhh!" Bauer said. "You'll be all right with her here."

Hilda turned a suspicious, tear-stained face at them all.

"Relax!" Bauer cautioned her again. "There are fifteen policemen around the apartment. If anybody tries anything, we'll have him in ten seconds."

"It would only take five for him to bury that ax in me." Hilda shuddered. "How would you like to walk those streets—knowing those eyes are looking at you—and at any minute he's going to jump out and—"

"Well, you're safe now," Bauer said.

"Safe?"

Hilda drank from a short glass. She had forsaken beer for whiskey. Her face, under the dull reddish glow, looked grotesque.

"You'd better get back to the window," Bauer said. "You've been away long enough."

Hilda stared at them as though they had gone out of their minds.

"And lower your strap, Hilda," Steinman said. "You want to attract him."

Hilda pushed down the line of her dress. The breast was exposed. Stark fear in her eyes, she screwed up a static, frigid smile on her deep red lips. She crossed her legs and leaned on the window sill. A cold breeze blew in through the smashed window frame, chilling her.

"Must I?" Hilda pleaded weakly.

Bauer ignored her.

A man's creaking shoes could be heard coming from a hallway in the interior of the building, closer to the door now.

"He's definitely *inside*, Martin," Steinman said.

Bauer nodded. He looked back at the Israeli woman. Not fear, but a strange and intense curiosity filled her eyes. Bauer marveled at her composure. He motioned her back farther into the shadow under the curtains.

The footsteps stopped, perhaps twenty meters away.

Steinman drew his revolver and stood behind the door. Then he turned slowly to Bauer with a strange expression on his face.

"It stopped."

Bauer put up a hand for silence. They waited and waited for the sound to recommence. But nothing.

With a look of disbelief, the Chief Inspector came forward. He took the pocket radio from Steinman.

"Koenig," Bauer whispered. "If the creaking shoes belong to you, tap once on the radio."

There was a tiny click of the radio transmitter, then a solitary tap, and then a click as the transmitter was turned off.

Bauer shook his head slowly.

"Koenig, if I hear anything from you again, I will have you washing cars the rest of your life. If you understand me, tap once on the radio."

There was another click, a feeble tap, then the click, and silence again.

They exhaled as one, and relaxed. Steinman went back to his position at the opposite corner where he could cover both the window and the door.

Hilda Dorn sat as before, a frigid smile plastered on her face. Fear shone through like a dark fire. Bauer looked at her sympathetically, but said nothing.

As the time passed, Madeline came slowly out of the shadow. She sat down against the wall, her sweater draped loosely across the shoulders, and her long legs at an angle. The street lamps hit her face with a long, slanted ray, throwing dark shadows across her cheeks, under her eyes. Across from her, the Inspector was poised, observing Hilda through a space in the curtain.

"Who was he talking about?" Madeline whispered.

"Who?"

"The Colonel."

There was no response.

"Who could he have killed?" Madeline asked.

"Hitler. He was secretary to a member of the staff."

Madeline's smile was filled with irony.

"The old man feels recriminations?"

"It's possible."

The Inspector, his handsome face crossed by lines of age and lack of sleep, ignored the smile. But he felt her eyes upon him.

"Secretary to which member of the staff?" she asked.

"Von Rundstedt."

133

"The Colonel must have wielded a good deal of responsibility," she said.

The ironic, dark smile never left her lips. It seemed to cut into the Inspector.

"I never discussed it with him," Bauer said.

They fell silent. The hour approached midnight. Hilda began to slump over, the crude, mechanical smile still afixed to her mouth. Steinman shifted his weight to his other leg and wearily stroked the barrel of his gun. Bauer and Madeline lay against opposite walls.

"Quiet!" Bauer said suddenly.

From the depths of the building, a creaking sounded along the empty corridors.

"I'll break him," Bauer muttered angrily. "I'll break him, I swear to you, I'll break him!"

He took Steinman's radio.

"Koenig, is that you? Tap once if you are moving."

There was no response.

"Answer me, Koenig. If you are walking around, tap the radio."

The radio clicked, and clicked off. There was no tap.

Steinman leaped to his feet and pressed himself behind the door. He held the gun out at an angle. Bauer pushed Madeline into the shadows again, and motioned the wakened Hilda to keep quiet. Bauer crouched down among the shattered pieces of glass, revolver drawn, poised and facing the door. In total darkness, all eyes were fixed on the door.

Footsteps hesitated, then shuffled closer to the door. They stopped.

Bauer held the revolver steady in two hands. Steinman pressed himself as flat as he could against the wall, and did not breathe.

The door knob was moved. The door began to open. A man's head began to appear. A round, limpid face with a square mustache and hair falling in the eyes poked itself in. It smiled.

"Hello, Hilda. Busy tonight?"

Steinman leaped upon him, knocking him against the doorpost. Bauer ran forward as he fell, and kicked the legs out from underneath him. The body crashed to the floor.

Steinman fell upon the man's chest. Bauer found the arm and pushed the thumb up and in, and the arm followed and was locked behind the back. The man had offered no resistance. He lay there like a sack of wet flour. Steinman sat on his chest and shone a flashlight on his face.

A sallow, whitened face with its little mustache twitching looked up unbelievingly at the inspectors.

"Winkler!" Hilda laughed. She laughed hysterically. "It's only Winkler!"

The little man under Steinman looked up like a cold fish. He smiled abjectly. The mustache moved regularly, to the right and to the left. The flower in his lapel was crushed.

"Little Winkler!" Hilda howled. There were tears in her eyes. She bent over where she stood, looking down at him. Even Winkler tried to join in the joke, but when Steinman looked at him again, he abruptly stopped.

"You know him?" Bauer said.

"Yes. Of course. He's nobody."

Winkler tried to raise himself to his elbows.

"What is this?" he demanded.

"We are the police," Bauer said.

Winkler fell back again.

"The police?— It's no crime in Munich— It's authorized— I often come here—to talk—"

"At this hour?" Bauer asked.

"I couldn't sleep. It often happens. Ask Hilda."

Hilda nodded, drained of the strength to laugh any more. She flopped weakly into her chair again and covered her face with a hand.

"What should we do with him, Martin?" Steinman asked.

"Get off his chest, I suppose."

"Why don't you let me go?" Winkler pleaded. "I promise I'll never come here again. My word as a man of— Oh, my God! If my wife ever finds out about this—"

Bauer pressed his face close to Winkler's.

"Look, Winkler," Bauer said. "If I let you go this time, do you promise to walk—not run—down the street and go directly home?"

Winkler raised his right hand.

"As God is my witness, Captain, I promise!"

Bauer scrutinized him a moment.

"All right," Bauer said. "Sit over there for a few minutes. Then you can go."

Bauer stood up. He sighed.

"And remember to walk, not run!"

"I'll remember! Bless you, sir!"

Steinman was grinning. Hilda had a renewed attack of laughter. Madeline stood beside the Inspector now, smiling in spite of herself. The Inspector began to blush.

"Winkler," Bauer muttered to himself in disgust.

After five minutes, in which Winkler sat with his hands on his knees at the wall beside the door, looking around like a lost puppy dog, Bauer raised a hand as a signal for him to leave.

"Yes, sir, thank you, sir. Thank you."

Winkler stepped out of the room backward, bowing profusely. The door closed and his footsteps slowly disappeared down the corridors.

Bauer and Steinman sat against the wall. Hilda once again was made to take her post in the overstuffed chair. Madeline sat near the shadows, but there was sufficient light for the two men to glance at her from time to time. Her form was pleasing to them in the soft, shadowed light where she sat. Her long legs and slender ankles made her look, despite the simplicity of her dress, in the height of fashion.

Madeline, in turn, had ample time to study the two police-men. Tired, their eyes darkened and faces drawn, she won-dered when they had slept last.

In the silence, the inspectors, the Israeli, and the prostitute sat, waiting, listening, watching each other now and then, and wandering each in his own thoughts from time to time.

"We'll be here all night," Madeline said.

"He probably won't come at all," Steinman said. "Not now."

Bauer closed his eyes.

"No. Not now," he agreed. "Whoever he is, I'm sure he's made other arrangements for the night. . . ."

*   *   *

A street-sweeping machine threw its orange light over the con-struction site. The maw of a great caterpillar appeared wildly in the dark and then disappeared again. Steel girders lay on the ground in piles as their shadows fluttered down their sides. There was no one about. From a small shack came the light of a single bulb.

The night watchman was an old man; the lines on his face had deepened until they resembled a mask. He looked out from his window, supporting himself on his pencil-thin arms. There was nothing, only shadows among the shadows. A cool, dry breeze disturbed the long grass still left on the site. The light bulb rocked back and forth overhead, throwing shadows vividly around the room.

He turned up his radio and returned to his newspaper. Around him on the walls were pictures of women with large breasts.

Crrrack!

Suddenly, a door smashed in across the yard. The night watch-man grabbed his lantern and turned on the battery.

"Who's there?" he asked nervously.

There was silence. His ears strained. The old man leaned out of the frail wooden doorway.

"Go home," he said. "There's no carnival here."

The battery beam followed over the dirt and stones, poking over the rusted wire and empty buckets lined up at the ditches. The red flags waved on strings in the night breeze.

Crrrack!

A door splintered, and the pieces flew out onto the dirt. Unbelieving, the old man stared. His fingers crawled at the snap on the leather pistol holster at the belt, but they only trembled and fumbled uselessly for the gun.

"Who's there?" he said. "What do you want?"

Suddenly, out of the depths of the utility hut, eyes emerged, caught and blinded in the beam of the battery light. The old man backed away, tripping backward over the buckets in the dirt. He fell, and the light beam shot up over his head.

"Leave me!" the old man screamed.

With a bound, the form from the hut bent low and ran past the night watchman on the ground, carrying in his arms heavy bundles. The old man turned and watched him go, adroitly, over the dirt piles and into the alley.

Cautiously, he picked himself up. He approached the disintegrated hut. Now he pulled his gun out and pointed it around the storehouse. Boxes of belts, nails, wires, and clippers were torn open. On the ground was a long, dented butcher's cleaver. The night watchman stared at it. It glinted back at him. The old man backed away.

He backed away slowly, his light beam protecting him, until he arrived at his shack. Once there, he closed the thin wooden door and locked it. He rubbed his cracked lips a moment, then inserted a thin, trembling finger into the dial of the telephone.

"Two complete cases," the night watchman whispered. "High explosives. And we are not registered to keep them here. I thought it best to call you before the police." He listened for instructions, looking nervously about. "Yes, sir, you can count on me, sir. I have seen and heard nothing."

He hung up. The moths, gathering once more on the swinging light bulb, threw fluttering shadows on the engraved, mask-like face below them.

MUNICH:
The Eleventh Day of Oktoberfest

CHAPTER TWELVE

Hilda Dorn sat leaning against the venetian blinds. She snored, but her eyes were half open.

Bauer and Madeline sat opposite each other. Madeline looked up at the ceiling, contemplative. A cathedral tower tolled the hour. It was five o'clock.

"It will be light soon," Madeline said.

"Yes," Bauer said.

"What do we do then?"

"Go home. We'll return again at night."

"And Hilda?"

"She'll sleep in jail."

Madeline sighed, nearly a yawn. Her head rested against the wall. She seemed comfortable, though it was only the effect of weariness.

"Poor man," she said.

"Who?"

"Whoever he is."

Bauer did not reply.

"To hide by day and kill by night," Madeline continued.

Across the room, Steinman pulled himself awake. He looked at the Chief Inspector, but the Inspector did not see him. The Chief Inspector was watching Madeline as she spoke.

> "I saw you in a dream—and know no day
> Shines in your night at all. I know so well.
> I saw the snake gnaw your heart away.
> I saw, my dear, how deep you are in hell."

Bauer smiled at Madeline. She had quoted it nearly perfectly. "Heinrich Heine," he said.

"Yes."

"You like Heine?"

She shrugged.

"I couldn't sleep. I found him among your books."

"Ahh. I see."

"I was surprised to find him there."

Bauer raised a quizzical eyebrow.

"Really? How so?"

"You burned his books."

"No. Not I. The other element."

"Still. He was destroyed."

"But his thoughts could never be destroyed."

"I wonder," she said. "So many things that were lovely perished in the war."

*　　*　　*

The Colonel awakened suddenly, a half-empty brandy glass in his hand.

Sunbeams penetrated the curtains of his home. He had fallen

asleep in his deep-cushioned leather chair. Sometime in the night, his wife had placed a woolen blanket over his legs. Now the chess pieces and brandy decanter shone with an eerie glow under the curtains beside his arm. He was perspiring heavily along his forehead, and with his handkerchief he gently mopped his brow. He opened his shirt so that the subtle breeze coming in through the window might cool his exposed chest.

The Colonel had had a dream. It was not a simple dream.

In his dream, the Colonel sat within an Officers' Club, reading the general orders. A small glass of brandy had dispersed the gloom of the night. No one else was around. In fact, the club seemed unusually large and dark.

General von Rundstedt came in, wandering among the tables toward Schuckert. He seemed not to know what he was doing, though when he saw Schuckert, he increased his speed and came directly toward him.

Before Colonel Schuckert could rise to his feet, the General sank and embraced Schuckert's legs.

"Forgive me," Von Rundstedt said, trembling. "Forgive me!"

Colonel Schuckert looked quickly around him, to ascertain that no one was watching.

"What is it, sir?" Schuckert said uncomfortably. "What's wrong?"

But the General began to weep, and only repeated, "Forgive me! Forgive me!"

Schuckert felt with revulsion the man's weight upon his knees.

"Come, come, sir," Schuckert said. "Discipline yourself. What are you talking about?"

Normally, Schuckert was not the sort of secretary one displayed one's emotions to. The Colonel was touched, yet baffled.

"Give me your pistol!" Von Rundstedt whispered hoarsely.

"No, sir. That is—you're not in your right mind. I can't do that. Best that you get a hold on yourself."

143

Just then, footsteps sounded in the far corridor of the Officers' Club.

Von Rundstedt looked around wildly, then tore himself from Schuckert and ran from the approaching footsteps, out of the door.

Colonel Count Claus von Stauffenberg walked in slowly, erectly, and stiffly. He, too, approached Schuckert and stood above him. He held up a hand, signifying: Do not rise.

"Well, Schuckert. We have failed."

"I'm sorry, sir. I am unable to understand—"

"He has triumphed again."

Colonel Count von Stauffenberg handed Schuckert his own pistol.

"Shall you or shall I?" he said.

"Please, sir—!"

"Never mind. I am no coward. I shall do it myself."

More footsteps sounded in the outer corridor. Von Stauffenberg's face turned white.

"Do you suppose it can be—? Already? Never mind. I am prepared."

The Colonel Count walked quickly, though with painful dignity, out the door through which Von Rundstedt had run.

Schuckert remained alone in the dark club. The general orders remained unread. As the footsteps approached, Schuckert's face twitched in anxiety and confusion.

Seconds later, General Friedrich Olbricht entered.

The General saluted in an ironic manner. Formality thus let down, the Colonel approached the General.

The General was looking at himself in the mirror at the side wall. He turned to Schuckert and smiled ruefully.

"The bomb, Schuckert."

"What, sir?"

"It was too weak."

"That's a pity, sir."

"Yes. Very much so."

The Colonel had only a dim notion of what the General spoke.

"His leg is injured," General Olbricht said. He turned away from Schuckert and laughed. "Only his leg."

The General adjusted his coat on which numerous ribbons decorated the chest.

"The man is charmed," the General said. "Quite charmed."

"Yes, sir."

"In any case, he is coming soon. I suppose Von Rundstedt and the others are out in the back?"

"Yes, sir."

"Quite so. I suspect it will be over soon. The Führer's personal execution squad, after all, is chosen with scrupulous care."

The Colonel stood, wide-eyed in bewilderment. General Olbricht placed an arm on the Colonel's shoulder.

"Learn from this, Schuckert. Learn and do well."

"Yes, sir."

General Olbricht saluted in mock formality, and walked out slowly through the club, his footsteps echoing, dimly and more dimly, in the dark.

Colonel Schuckert went to his table and poured himself a large brandy. His mind was reeling as he swallowed the burning, pleasant amber liquid. The darkness seemed to expand on all sides of him, until he was standing in a circle of light surrounded by a vast, black void.

Footsteps came slowly down the hall.

The feet were encased in new, creaking boots. They limped, one leg favored, down the hall. The footsteps came steadily forward, until the sound reverberated in Schuckert's mind like hammer blows, bringing him back to consciousness.

Awakening from his nightmare, the Colonel turned and, still holding his glass of brandy, hurried out the side door into the chill morning street.

145

The dawn was now breaking over Munich. The clouds which had threatened rain over the Oktoberfest for the last week had retreated. They were pulling apart in front of the sun. In a red glow over the hills, the dawn was bursting into the city.

Colonel Schuckert stood on the street, looking surreptitiously around him. No one was about except a lone street cleaner. The shops were still closed, the bars drawn up to protect the windows, and the fresh air which circulated through the deserted streets cleared the Colonel's mind.

He threw the brandy glass into a vacant lot and began to walk quickly. He straightened his uniform as best he could and continued down the Rhumfordstrasse. He required mental discipline now; there were men and an organization to command. His footsteps resounded crisply on the pavement as he marched down to the Hall of Justice.

The great hall had turned pink in the beginning rays of day. The Colonel stepped briskly up the stone stairs and smartly saluted an inspector who descended the stairs, carrying a briefcase under the arm.

"Good morning, Colonel," said the desk clerk, with surprise. "Your wife has been somewhat worried about you, sir, and asks you to return her call."

"Thank you," the Colonel mumbled.

He reached out for, and received, the log of the last night's activity. He noticed that the stakeout of the prostitute's room was still being conducted. In the bright lights, surrounded by the security of many men in uniform in a smoothly run organization, the Colonel found himself at home.

He stood, reading the log, under the flag of the Federal Republic.

"Colonel Schuckert!"

The Colonel looked up. His eyes focused on a thin, energetic man who came striding down the brightly lit corridor.

"Oh, it's you, Flanck."

Flanck paused in front of him, excitement in his eyes, breathing hard from the exertion of running half the way.

"Good morning, Colonel. We are the early ones, aren't we?"

"What is it, Flanck?"

The Colonel walked leisurely, Flanck alongside him, surveying the various rooms of interrogation, the conferences, the laboratory, taking note of men and time schedules.

"I learned this morning that Inspector Bauer has instructed the Force not to use arms."

"Unless personally endangered. That is his prerogative."

"But this is madness. The man is insane."

"Nevertheless," the Colonel said dryly, "Bauer has the authority." And then, more softly, "I think he has a personal interest in saving the man."

The Colonel and Flanck stopped outside an interrogation room. The room was empty, bars of sunlight coming in through the venetian blinds, shedding patterns of light against the white walls and tiled floors.

"I have rescinded the order," Flanck said.

The Colonel's head moved back slightly.

"I am in charge of this case, Flanck—"

"But the danger—"

"—and for now, Bauer has my authority!"

The Colonel began to walk on.

"Shall you change the order back again," Colonel Schuckert said, "or shall I?"

Flanck double stepped to catch up to Schuckert.

"I will not expose Munich to this sort of danger—"

"The order is as before," the Colonel said, walking patiently down the hall.

Flanck had to walk faster to keep up.

"I'll have you know, Colonel, that I have reached an agreement on this with His Honor, the Mayor."

"Without speaking to me first? You work fast, Flanck."

147

"I repeat, Colonel: His Honor and I have an understanding."

"I don't doubt it."

They entered a large hall where the light cast itself evenly and created no shadows. Men went by in both directions, in uniform and out, busily, heading for their stations, or coming off their night duty.

"What does the Colonel mean by that remark?"

"That the politics of His Honor are well known."

Flanck's face tightened somewhat.

"If the Colonel is referring to a few unfortunate choices for the council—"

"Yes, Flanck. Men of proven experience, isn't that what he called them?"

"Men whose expertise was badly needed."

"As you like, Flanck."

Flanck walked around the Colonel, forcing him to stop. The hallway was suddenly deserted.

"The war is over, Colonel. Germany is rebuilt. Rebuilt. You can't keep her in moral rubble any more."

"*I* never put her there, Herr Flanck."

The Colonel gently pushed the District Attorney aside as he continued down the hall. Flanck's face was white. But the Colonel merely put his hands behind his back and walked calmly down the hall.

"Oh, didn't you?" Flanck shouted. "Didn't you indeed? And who, if not the likes of you?"

The words pierced the Colonel to the heart. His face drew at the sound of them. His nightmare came back to him. He turned slowly to address himself to Flanck, and saw Koenig standing in a doorway, having heard the entire exchange.

"What is it, Koenig?" Colonel Schuckert said. "It had best be important, what you have to say."

Koenig looked at Colonel Schuckert, and then at Flanck. Not

daring to exclude one or the other, he looked one way, and then the other.

"The bathhouse on the Isar, sirs," he said. "It's been bombed. All units have been called."

CHAPTER THIRTEEN

Flames leaped up on the beams and turned the brick walls red. The Isar River boiled and fumed. Pipes and bricks fell over into the water, and rapids quickly formed and re-formed, running through the fallen elements. Neighbors and passers-by quickly gathered. Sirens wailed along the river front.

"What happened?"

"Was anybody hurt?"

"The superintendent. Scalded to death."

"The river must have backed in."

So the voices murmured.

The hanging walls, standing like the ruins of Babylon, teetered over the twisted wreckage of pipes and boilers, bits of tile, and shredded papers and towels. A large brick building, the great bathhouse on the Isar had stood for centuries, like a citadel over the riverbanks. And through its doors, summer and winter, on alternate nights, came the male and female citizens of Munich. Few homes were equipped with private baths in Europe, and the public bathhouse was a necessary adjunct to cleanliness. The water of the river was channeled into pipes and boilers, long parallel tubing feeding the rows upon rows of shower stalls and steam rooms. Throughout the day and evening, people would stroll in and, in the luxury of communal steam, converse, relax, and regain their mental health. Over their heads were glazed tiles; around the doors white figurines fondly gazed down upon them. Huge chambers and antechambers led into waiting rooms and linen rooms, so that when the explosion ripped through the brick and plaster, the elegant façade of the great bathhouse was peeled away like the lid of a sardine tin, revealing room upon shattered room, spewing steam into the cold air of the morning.

Martin Bauer stopped the car. Madeline and Steinman stared out at the eerily glowing wreck. Smoke still billowed out of the foundations. Firemen, obscured in the blue smoke, went head down into the bowels of the old building, dragging hoses after them. All the spectators seemed awed, and they stood, their necks craned, to see the glow of red flickering against the rising smoke.

"Excuse me," Bauer said. "Stay in the car. I'll see what happened."

But Steinman and Madeline quickly clambered out of the car to watch the activity. A wall came crashing down, and a row of shower heads fell into a wet dust, gleaming and shining in the early morning sun.

The Inspector strode through the citizens gathered at the edge of the rope stretched across the periphery of the disaster. He ducked under the rope.

Fire engines dominated all access routes, hoses falling over curbs and running through the piles of hot bricks and mortar.

Firemen rushed past the Inspector, dragging out smoldering timbers and twisted pieces of pipe. A fine spray drenched him, turning his dark suit even darker.

"Bauer!"

Bauer turned.

Out of the shadow of the curling smoke, a form appeared, and a voice familiar to him. Hugo Flanck lit a cigarette.

"Who do you think did this?" Flanck went on smoothly. "Someone with a grudge against towels?"

Firemen in asbestos suits and gas masks appeared through the densest parts of the smoke. They carried several gallon cans of smoking debris. Overturning the cans onto the ground, they began sorting through the smoking coals.

"Dynamite," said one of the firemen. "In three sections of the bathhouse so far."

Bauer looked over the steaming ruins. The long corridors, down which the men had marched one day and the women the next, stood now, half exposed, still white and sterile in parts.

"Incredible, isn't it?" Flanck said.

Bauer did not look at the District Attorney.

"Which reminds me to ask you, Bauer. Did your killer bother to show up?"

"No, sir. He never came."

"I thought not." Flanck threw his cigarette away. It blended with the glowing, pulsating embers on the ground. "There will be a conference this afternoon in my chambers," he said. "Certain ramifications of your case will be discussed."

Flanck turned and slowly walked away, keeping an eye on the burning debris underfoot. He passed under the rope at the perimeter of the crowd and disappeared.

A fireman pushed his way past Bauer, hauling a half section of water tank, split in two by the blast, with wires of a valve bobbing oddly on the end.

"An incredible amount, sir," the fireman said, shaking his head. "An incredible amount."

Bauer caught sight of the massive form of Colonel Schuckert directing the fire patrol around the far corner of the lot. Two sergeants stood behind him, each with matters to urgently report. Bauer, with much difficulty, pulled his way over the smoking debris.

Bundles of towels, like dead bodies, had been strewn over the ground. Now they smoked. Bits of blue rose up out of them, the rags inside smoldering, and the yard filled with the curled and outstretched forms.

The Colonel finished his instructions and now stood, with a pensive expression on his face, appearing not to notice Bauer at his side. After a moment, the Colonel turned.

"Flanck spoke to you?"

"Yes, sir."

The Colonel looked at him closely.

"You haven't slept all night, have you?"

"No, sir."

"I suggest you get some. Flanck has called a conference for this afternoon."

Bauer looked closely at the Colonel's sympathetic face. The Colonel's face was terribly drawn, composed, but twitching at the side of the mouth. A dark, lost expression was in his eyes.

"Yes, sir," Bauer said. "He told me."

Bauer and Colonel Schuckert watched the activity a moment. It proceeded smoothly, as all units had been dispatched to their assignments. Steinman and Madeline, standing beside the police car across the yard, watched the fire, too. The sunlight now bathed them with a full and yellow glow.

"I believe he will speak to the Ministry about the case," Colonel Schuckert said. "As I feared from the beginning, this will reach the ears of Bonn."

The Colonel brushed a bit of black soot from his uniform.

"I was ever mindful of that possibility, sir."

"Perhaps it will come out right," the Colonel said vaguely, and without nod or salute he turned and walked away toward the cluster of fire trucks.

Bauer watched after him thoughtfully.

He walked slowly back to his police car. Steinman and Madeline watched him as he approached. They tried to judge the expression on his face. But the Inspector only got into the car and put a hand over his eyes, closing them, bone tired.

"Shall we go, Paul?"

Steinman helped Madeline in. Steinman drove. Madeline drew her sweater about her and closed her eyes. The burning embers shot up into the early morning, over their heads, and the car slowly pulled away from the bricks in the yard.

Inspector Bauer leaned back in his seat.

"There will be a conference this afternoon," he said. "You needn't come, if you are sleeping."

Steinman looked at the Chief Inspector.

"Flanck?" Steinman asked.

Bauer nodded. He looked out the window, unable to sleep. An old woman, her hair in a bun, was smiling and watering the peonies that grew high around her white fence.

In the back seat, Madeline had fallen into a light, troubled sleep.

"It won't be so bad," Steinman said. "Now he has another case to occupy his ambitions."

The Inspector grunted in agreement.

The oak trees and the maple, which lined the streets, shone in the morning light, reflected in frosty crystals of morning dew.

"Unless it is the same man, I suppose," Bauer muttered. "But that doesn't make sense. What could he have against a bathhouse?"

The Chief Inspector slumped down in his seat, half awake as the car bumped over a series of railroad tracks.

In the back of the car, Madeline turned in uneasy sleep.

Images of the fire burned in her brain, great billows of smoke extending up from the bricks and shadowing the mounds of towel bags lying all over the yard. Billows of flames ate out the wood among the brick, and standing like a row of sentries, the upturned row of shower heads gleamed and then slowly blackened as the hubbub of German voices hung like a drone over the compound.

*   *   *

"You mean the same man did it?" Flanck's outraged voice broke the stillness of the conference room.

"I—I don't know what you're talking about," stammered the night watchman. The lines of his face were screwed into a parody of fear, a mask of bewilderment and mortification. "I really don't, sir."

Colonel Schuckert, Bauer, and Steinman had regained their sleep, and now sat refreshed, immaculately dressed, glaring at the old man, still in his work clothes.

Madeline, on the other side of the table, looked at him with pity.

"I'll tell you what I'm talking about," Flanck said. "Someone walked off with a case and a half of dynamite, leaving a butcher's cleaver behind—and you didn't report it!"

"But I did. When my relief showed up."

"Eight o'clock this morning. Don't they give you a telephone over there?"

The night watchman's face screwed up even further, but all he met were the blank, impassive stares of the assembled group.

"Don't you read the newspapers?" Flanck went on. "Haven't you heard that there's a maniac loose in Munich, chopping people to bits with that—?"

Flanck pointed to the table.

155

There, lying on a dark towel, was the butcher's cleaver. The blade was dented, and the end of the handle splintered. It lay there like a cold, metallic fish, under the fluorescent lights.

"Well, speak!"

The watchman grew visibly frightened.

"I—I had no idea. I thought it was children. . . . They come around every night and bother me . . . I thought surely it was them . . . stealing rope . . ."

Flanck, disgusted, gave up on him. Bauer took the opportunity to lean forward.

"You saw nothing?" Bauer said quietly. "The face, the clothes? Anything?"

"No. Only a shadow. I thought it was the children."

Flanck drummed his fingers on the table, thinking. He was clearly finished with the old man.

"All right," Bauer said. "Go home. Stay there. We may want to talk to you again."

The night watchman's face curved in a different direction, attempting a smile.

"Thank you," he said. He rose stiffly from his chair. Steinman moved his own chair to let him pass. The old man bowed his way toward the door. "Thank you. Thank you."

He left. The door closed. The room was silent but for the air conditioning overhead.

Flanck sighed. "He has turned in his ax for something worse."

They turned to look at him, but his own dark eyes were fixed on the butcher's cleaver in the middle of the table. The cruel, hard weight of the blade seemed to hold his attention rigidly. All eyes went toward the weapon.

"His motives for killing those people," Colonel Schuckert said, "we can understand. Insane, yet logical. But a building?" he said incredulously. "Mortar and brick?" He looked up questioningly. "What possible crime could *it* have committed? A bathhouse . . ."

Madeline leaned forward. Her eyes were stark, her voice a whisper.

"They marched them into the building. The sign on one side said 'Men' and on the other, 'Women.' They crowded them into the shower stalls, undressed, and closed a heavy steel door. Then they turned on the faucets from the outside and, instead of water, Cyklon B gas came out. It was poison. It burned their lungs. It was hot like lime. Naturally, there were no windows, no ventilation. It was airtight. They would bunch up near the bottom of the door, hoping for a bit of air.

Madeline looked at Bauer, who swallowed. Flanck had paled.

"You don't think—?" Colonel Schuckert asked. His mind was unwilling to absorb what she was saying.

"Then they transported them by conveyor belt," Madeline went on. "They crowded the bodies onto the belts, and from there they were thrown into the furnaces. Sometimes they were not yet dead. They cremated them as quickly as possible, but there was always a backlog of bodies. The stench was awful. It could be smelled ten kilometers into the country—"

"Really!" Flanck interposed. "For what reason is this sort of—"

"Because," Madeline continued, "anything that has a conveyor belt is his target. Anything made of brick with smokestacks, lime kilns, morgues. Because he thought the bathhouse was the shower stall, he destroyed it!"

"Totally preposterous!" Flanck exclaimed.

"It could be true, Herr Flanck," Bauer said cautiously. "The janitor was found stuffed in a furnace."

"And the butcher's shop?" Flanck said. "I suppose—"

"Why not?" Madeline demanded. "Bodies on meathooks. Why not? They did worse. Instruments and tools, never designed for use on humans—"

"Enough, Miss Kress!"

"Herr Flanck," Bauer said. "The point is that all these places are in danger. If the man is . . . hallucinating, or whatever . . ."

"Hospitals," Madeline said.

"Hospitals?" Flanck said.

"Doctors. Needles. The clinics. Wearing white coats. They injected poisons, kerosene, chemicals. To watch them die. Boys shriveled up in front of them. Sexual experiments—women were operated on, castrations, tortures with wire and glass—all under the cover of 'medical work.' Do you think this man won't be struck with the sight of a hospital?"

"My God, yes!" Steinman put in. "Bakers, Herr Flanck. The ovens."

"Or the Army or the police," Colonel Schuckert cautiously added. "The uniforms, I mean. Do you think just because the uniform is a nice pleasant green now it makes them look or sound so different?"

There was a terrible silence.

"How long can we wait?" the Colonel finally said, "until he's brought Munich crumbling about our heads? If this man can mistake innocent people for the SS—and an innocuous bathhouse for—for those horrible places—" The Colonel's eyes were locked onto the shine of the metal blade sitting on the table. "Where will he stop?"

"I don't know," Bauer said.

Flanck suddenly leaned forward.

"All right, Bauer. What *do* you know?"

"Sir?"

"You know that Miss Kress has a right to insinuate all these things. You know the killer is out after Nazis. You know the janitor is Tauber and the butcher is Goering. But when it comes down to prescribing effective means of stopping this man, you seem particularly impotent. Except, of course, of staying the night, revolvers drawn, in a whore's room."

"Just a minute, Herr Flanck," Bauer said.

"Dredging up your photographs, showering us with these horrible implications. You disgrace—"

"To hell with your disgrace, Flanck!"

Bauer rose angrily. Flanck followed him up, eying him steadily.

"Gentlemen," Flanck said. "This brings us to the real point of this conference. Colonel Schuckert, I believe you know this case has been mishandled from the beginning. Inspector Bauer is obviously incompetent."

"My competence has *never* been questioned until this case," Bauer returned heatedly.

"It's true," Colonel Schuckert said. He, too, had risen, in an effort to maintain calm. "Bauer's record is formidable."

"For the last time," Flanck said, "I suggest you replace him."

"Your *suggestion*, Herr Flanck," the Colonel said dryly, "shall receive my consideration."

Flanck gazed steadily at Colonel Schuckert.

He gazed around the room, at Bauer who angrily stared back, at Steinman who was embarrassed by the whole affair, and then back at Bauer. For Flanck, Madeline did not even exist.

"Very well," Flanck said. "I understand."

Flanck picked up his briefcase and moved away. He arched his neck stiffly. Composed, he smiled ingratiatingly.

"Good day, gentlemen."

Flanck strode from the room. Again the door closed on a departing figure.

Colonel Schuckert sighed. It seemed to signify the end of the conference. Steinman rose, too.

"What will happen now?" Madeline asked.

The Colonel spoke softly, enunciating clearly and pleasantly. "He will go to Bonn, where he will tell all manner of tales about Inspector Bauer and myself, and succeed in having the case transferred to his own authority."

Bauer's face was thoughtful.

"I'm sorry, Bauer," Colonel Schuckert said, "but I'm afraid you will be relieved."

No one moved for a while, or spoke.

"As for you, Miss Kress, what your role, if any, will be, I can't prophesy," the Colonel said. "Your assistance thus far has been invaluable. I hope you can stay." He bowed slightly.

As they congregated around the door, the Colonel fitted his cap to his head.

"Flanck has a penchant for guns," Colonel Schuckert said. "I'd say you have about two days, thanks to the bureaucracy of Bonn, to try to find your killer and take him alive."

The Chief Inspector nodded a short, decisive bow.

BONN:
The Twelfth Day of Oktoberfest

CHAPTER FOURTEEN

Madeline walked under a poster of the Holy Land. The blue sky shone in eternal depth over the rugged peaks of the Sinai. Madeline paused. Behind her, the golden Dome of the Rock glittered over the ancient, sacred hills of Jerusalem.

"Excuse me," she said, in Hebrew. "I haven't much time."

At the desk, a handsome young man looked up and then rose. He smiled and gestured for her to sit.

"Please," he said in Hebrew. "I am Eli Krafft."

Madeline handed to him her documents from the Archives.

"Madeline," he said as he read through them, "I am honored." He handed back the documents.

She studied the young man. He leaned back, frankly returning her look.

"The Embassy is at your disposal," he said.

"I came from Munich this morning. There is a man—he may be a Jew—" Madeline said. "I want him in Israel."

Eli raised an eyebrow.

"What's to prevent him from going?"

"He is a mental."

"He has no relatives?"

"I don't know."

"Who is he?"

Madeline paused.

Eli sensed some difficulty here. He gestured to the small cups on the table. She did not refuse, so he filled them slowly with thick, Arab-style coffee. He added sugar copiously. Steam wavered upward. Madeline watched the steam rise, and waited for the cup to cool.

"Who is he, Madeline?" Eli repeated.

"A criminal."

"Ahh. I see. That is a little more difficult."

"No. I have not made myself clear."

"Criminals can be deported. It has been done in the past. But not very easily. What is the crime?"

"Murder."

"There is no possibility, then."

"He is not caught, yet."

At this, Eli was stopped.

He sipped his coffee slowly, holding the cup between thumb and forefinger. He eyed the attractive woman carefully.

"I suspected this would be no ordinary day when I woke up," he smiled.

A secretary came into the office through a side door, carrying several envelopes. Without looking at her, Eli waved her back. Eli leaned forward.

"Who is he?" Eli asked.

"I don't know."

Madeline set down her coffee cup.

"Three men have been killed in Munich by a man with a butcher's knife. One looked like Goering, one like Himmler, and the third like Tauber, a *Rapportführer* at Auschwitz."

Eli said nothing.

"An attack was then made on a prostitute. She bore a resemblance to Juana Bormann."

"You are not mistaken?"

"No."

"I see. You are assisting Munich."

"Yes."

Eli said nothing again. He tapped his lips with his finger.

"And yesterday the municipal bathhouse was destroyed."

"I know," Eli said. He pointed to a small portable radio on his desk. "We heard about it."

"It was the same man."

Eli inhaled.

"They didn't tell us that," he said.

"They won't, either. Not for a while. They are suppressing the news as far as possible."

"Why?"

"The publicity would be undesirable," she said bitterly.

Eli nodded.

"How do you know he is a Jew?"

"Because nobody else would know those faces, those scenes."

Eli shrugged.

"Germans were there, too," he said.

"But it does not upset them."

"You don't believe that someone with a guilty conscience . . . ?"

"No. Impossible."

Eli brushed his hair back.

"I'm not sure what we can do," he said frankly. "If he is a German citizen . . ."

"But he is a Jew first."

"Yes," Eli protested, "but—"

"But what?"

"You can't just kidnap him. Assuming you find him. The days of the Eichmann affair are over."

"They will kill him, Krafft. The District Attorney wants him dead, quickly."

"Look, Madeline. If a Jew has committed these crimes, he will be tried and pronounced guilty or insane, as a German court wills it."

"But they will kill him," Madeline repeated. "German 'justice' is notoriously sensitive to international politics. And if silence is wanted . . ."

Eli stood up and looked out the window. The great industrial landscape stretched out to a gray and shining river. German automobiles and airplanes appeared in all directions on the ground and in the sky.

"It would be a very delicate position," he admitted.

"'Position'!" Madeline exploded. "What are you talking about?"

Eli turned around. Sympathetically, he looked at her.

"The war is over, Madeline. There are new realities now, new objectives. Israel and Germany are very close today."

"I'm not interested in economics."

"They exist, I'm afraid."

Madeline raised herself stiffly.

"Examine the question with the proper authorities, please," she said. "That's why I came today."

"Of course. But I can promise you nothing."

Madeline looked uncomfortably around the room.

"There is something else I want," she said.

"Yes?"

"There are a number of sources of wartime documentation which Yad Vashem has not yet microfilmed. I want to take a look at them before I leave."

"Certainly. I can put you in touch with them."

Madeline drank her coffee.

"We get our machine parts from Germany," she said, "for which we pay them in grapefruit. Do we also have to pay them in Jews?"

Eli softened.

"I will put your case in the strongest terms," he promised. "If he is not political, there may be a chance. . . ."

"I want him out of Germany," she concluded.

Eli inclined his head to one side. It meant: I shall try.

"Incredible, isn't it?" Madeline said. "Who would have thought we would come back so soon? And yet, here we are."

"Well, it's as they say," Eli said, somewhat relieved that the main part of the conversation seemed concluded. "Germany is a beautiful country. There is only one thing wrong with it."

"Germans."

Eli smiled. They walked together to the door.

"I leave you to your 'new realities,'" Madeline said.

"*Shalom.*"

"*Shalom.*"

She left. Eli watched her walk down the hall, then wait for the elevator. She stood there, lovely and determined. She had come from a different world, almost legendary to him now, the war generation. Abruptly as she had come into his office, she stepped into the open elevator, the doors closed, and she disappeared.

*   *   *

In Bonn, Flanck likewise sat in an office.

Not without first waiting, however. Flanck waited an interminable length of time. The Russians could have marched through lower Franconia, with time for tea and borscht, and returned in that length of time. For an hour and a quarter Flanck sat in his dark, neatly pressed suit, holding a briefcase on his lap.

Frank De Felitta

"The Minister will see you now," said the male secretary.

Flanck strode into the Minister's chamber.

"Herr Flanck," said the Minister, holding out both hands for a handshake. "Did you have an interesting trip?"

"Yes. I took the Bonn Express."

"Ahh. The New Electric."

"Indeed. One hundred and twenty kilometers an hour. A private business office. Private telephones. Fifty-seven cars."

"I shall have to take it."

The Minister gestured toward the chair.

The Minister did not remember Flanck. Yet, it was not the first time that Flanck had sat before him with a briefcase. They had been much younger, then. Of lower ranks. Under a different government.

"Will you have a cigar?"

Flanck's heart beat a little more rapidly. The inner chamber of ministers always did this to him. He surveyed the wood-paneled room, the painting of Adenauer upon the wall, the photograph of the Krupp summer residence, signed.

"Thank you, sir. I shall."

Flanck's head bent forward, almost in deference, as he suffered the Minister to light it for him. Flanck carefully noted the brand of the cigars.

The Minister blew the smoke from his nostrils. His white hair fairly glowed against the window.

"What is going on in Munich?" he asked bluntly.

"He continues to elude us."

"Why is that, Flanck?"

"The Chief Inspector is incompetent."

"Come, come, Flanck."

"In the face of all evidence to the contrary, he persists in the theory that—"

"Yes, yes," the Minister said with displeasure. "You told me by telephone."

Flanck scarcely dared raise his eyes to the Minister's.

The Minister continued.

"Yet, surely Schuckert—I know him by reputation—would not allow anything untoward to go on."

"The Colonel is totally under the domination of the Chief Inspector."

"How so, Flanck?"

"Dependence on brandy has eaten his judgment away."

Something about Flanck's weasel-like impatience pleased the Minister. For a fleeting moment the Minister had the impression that he had met Flanck somewhere before.

"I see, Flanck. I see. That, of course, is a very serious matter."

Flanck said nothing.

"What about the woman, Flanck?"

"A typical Israeli, sir."

"Damn."

The Minister lowered his hand to a glass dish which featured an engraved swan. He flicked his cigar ashes into it. Flanck, who had been wondering what to do with his own ash, now leaned forward and did the same.

"That is bad news, indeed," the Minister said.

Flanck pulled out a sheaf of photographs from his briefcase. Even at a quick glance the Minister knew what they were. He turned a shade paler. He looked like an older man suddenly.

"This is obscene!" he said to Flanck. "And the Colonel says nothing?"

"Nothing."

The Minister hastily sorted through the pictures of the lime pits, eaten-out photographs of obscure criminals of the Third Reich, bodies laid on top of each other, taken by photographers who had not been able to look closely at what they were photographing.

"This is the sort of thing the woman has been filling the Chief Inspector's mind with ever since she arrived. Upon trash such as this the investigation is being based. I have had to use all my limited power and persuasion to keep these pictures out of the newspapers."

The Minister picked up his telephone. He requested his secretary to enter immediately.

"I'm glad you showed these to me in person, Flanck."

Flanck bowed his head.

The young male secretary came in and sat down in a delicate way, and took a pad and pencil from his suit pocket.

The Minister dictated the form of the message. When he was through, he dismissed the secretary and looked up at Flanck.

"Have you been on the eastbound out of Hanover?" asked the aged Minister. "One hundred forty kilometers an hour in places. And a gourmet shop in the central car."

"Yes, sir," Flanck lied. "Often. One of my favorite lines."

Flanck left the Minister's chambers with an envelope in his pocket. There were a number of formalities which lay ahead. Essentially, however, the case was his.

MUNICH:
The Thirteenth Day of Oktoberfest

CHAPTER FIFTEEN

It was two o'clock. School had let out early in deference to the Oktoberfest.

The young girl dangled her schoolbooks across the rubble of the construction site, now and then permitting the bindings to brush against jutting rocks and shards of broken glass. It seemed less accidental than a conscious act of rebellion.

Each day, ever since the old tanning factory had been torn down, the girl had availed herself of this short cut to her home. Not that it saved her any time exactly, but it did provide her with a bit of adventure. And so, each day she would linger on her way, pausing to examine and explore among the hilly ruins of brick, lath, and mortar, her eyes constantly searching for new and interesting treasure. Two days before, she had found a wonderful piece of carved metal, which had turned out to be the

broken handle of a fine silver spoon. Even her father considered
it worth something. So, today, she picked her way especially
slowly over a new area of the excavation site—somewhat off her
regular route—in the hope of discovering something truly
remarkable.

It was just as she reached the apex of a mountain of bricks
that she spied the small window, half hidden in a section of low
wall which formed the base of a huge mound of debris.

The young girl quickly bent down to examine the window.
Half covered with piled dirt and rocks, the rectangular opening
was still large enough to permit a person to squeeze through.

She peered into the window, thrusting her head through the
opening and shielding her eyes with her hands to adjust her
sight to the darkness within. A cold, damp graveyard breath
exhaled up into her face, which, while slightly scary, also thrilled
her, as it conjured up images of treasure hoards in dank pirate
caves.

In a moment, the dim configurations of a small room came
into her view and, a few feet below her, an easy drop really, a
rock-strewn floor of broken concrete.

Gingerly, she eased her lean body through the window and
lowered herself to the floor. She paused, considered the problem
of her schoolbooks, which she had left outside by the window,
and decided it was safe to leave them there, as she certainly would
not be tarrying long in this gloomy cellar, since, among other
things, she was afraid of rats.

Gradually, her eyes began to see things more clearly in the
darkness. For example, a door suddenly appeared at the far end
of the small chamber. The threshold was piled high with rocks
and plaster chunks, and its opening was a good deal less than her
height but, she judged, easily negotiable. Carefully, she stepped
over rocks, lath sticks, and broken glass, avoiding sharp objects
such as rusty nails, once losing her footing and slipping back a

step, but eventually managing to conquer all of the obstacles in her path.

It was when she entered the next room that she began to hear the strange sound. At first she thought it came from rats, and her pulses quickened with terror. But then, as her eyes and ears adjusted to this new environment, she began to relax, as she realized that the sound was not rats at all but the heavy snoring of a sleeping person. Almost like the sounds that came from her parents' bedroom at night.

With some confidence now, the girl began to take tentative steps toward the familiar sound, testing each piece of ground ahead of her before committing her weight to it. It took quite some time for her to traverse the entire length of this room, which was a good deal larger than the first one.

Stepping across another threshold, which was entirely clear of debris, she saw, at the far end of a long, low corridor, a tiny culvert, made up of fallen beams, and a partial brick wall, its lathwork exposed. A ray of dusty daylight penetrated through a small opening in the lower part of the wall, sending a slash of light across the hunched-over figure of a sleeping man. He was snoring very loudly.

The girl waited a long moment before taking another step, and even considered leaving, when suddenly her eyes caught the glitter of something precious lying among some rocks beside the man's shoe.

He was still snoring soundly as the girl silently knelt before him and extended her fingers to the glittering object. Delicately seizing it between thumb and forefinger, she brought it to her eyes and studied it minutely. It was a small piece of red glass, possibly from a stained-glass window, for its deep ruby color glowed with warmth, exuding a richness that fairly dazzled the girl. It was a find, indeed.

So absorbed in the glass was she that she never realized the man had stopped snoring and that his eyes had snapped open and were observing her with maniacal intensity. It was only when the girl put the glass to her eyes and began to examine her red-hued surroundings that she saw the fear-ravaged eyes staring back at her.

"Hello," she said, smiling. "You were sleeping."

The man's hand slowly crept to a jagged rock at his side and clutched it purposefully.

"Look what I found," said the girl, extending the red glass toward him. "When you hold it to your eye, it makes the whole world red."

The man's burning eyes watched the girl as a cat watches a bird. His fingers tightened on the rock.

"Here, look through it. Please," begged the girl. "It's beautiful, really."

The man's eyes lost some of their intensity. His fingers, clutching the rock, relaxed somewhat.

Withdrawing the glass, the girl heaved a long, petulant sigh. "Well, if you don't want to, you don't have to."

"—Anna?" His voice was less human than animal.

"What?" asked the girl.

"Anna?" said the man, in a soft, broken whisper.

"Anna?" The girl giggled. "No. Not Anna. Freda."

The man's unblinking eyes gradually began filling with tears.

"Anna?" he beseeched.

"Not Anna. My name is Freda."

"Anna? Anna?" His voice was choked, his breathing had quickened noticeably.

The little game was beginning to frighten the girl. She rose haughtily.

"I'm not going to stay here if you call me Anna."

"Anna?" he pleaded hoarsely.

"There," the girl scolded, "you said it again!" And she began to back away down the corridor.

"Anna!" shouted the man, suddenly moving forward and grasping for the girl's dress. Screaming, the girl dropped the piece of glass and fled in a panic down the corridor, disappearing from his view.

"Anna!" he softly called after her, his eyes welling with tears, coursing down his dirt-encrusted face in a network of rivers.

"Anna," he sobbed. "Anna. Anna. Anna."

*   *   *

The conveyor belts run night and day in the big brick buildings. Gears and cranks stand upright under the rumbling rollers. A half light comes in through the dirt-streaked windows high in the lofts. The smoke pours out of the chimneys without cessation.

Laborers push the kegs down the belts, toward the platform from which the horse-drawn wagons supply themselves with the beer.

"Hey, Rudi!" the laborer whispered.

Rudi, washing down the metal chutes in the loft, looked up.

"What is it, Heins?"

Heins pointed down below. There, a small television set had been propped upon an overturned keg, and two chairs set up in front. Images flashed noisily onto the huge, empty storehouse floor. A man stood watching.

"Shhh!"

"What do you think he wants?"

"Maybe he's lost."

"He's sleepwalking."

"Ahh! Look! He likes the television set!"

Heins moved closer to Rudi, leaning on his broom. They watched the man below, wearing a blue shirt and slacks, cautiously peering at the television set, on all fours. He kept himself to the ground. When the image changed, he jerked around, and hid himself further into the dirt floor.

"You know what I think, Rudi?"

"What?"

"He's an idiot."

"An idiot?"

Rudi and Heins stared down. They both smiled.

"I've never seen an idiot before," Rudi said.

"Except for your brother-in-law."

Rudi poked Heins.

"No. A true idiot. Someone should come and get him."

"What's that in his hand?"

"Firecrackers, I think."

"He'll hurt himself."

"You go. I'll watch him."

"No. You go. I'll watch."

Down below them, directly under their feet, the man withdrew and hid himself behind a row of barrels. Plainly he was afraid to leave, for he kept looking toward the door, but every time the images changed, he threw himself down again.

"Go," Rudi said, with a threat in the tone of voice. "And I'll keep watch."

"Oh, all right. But don't chase him away."

Heins ducked his head and disappeared through a small door in the upper loft. Rudi could hear his footsteps softly disappear down the wooden ladder.

The man below was huge. He seemed to study the television, the wire, and the small antennae. He looked around from time to time, but nothing among the barrels of beer and metal chutes resembled what flashed onto the tiny blue screen.

Then, with a lunge, the man threw himself upon the television. With a barrel upraised in his arms, he ran forward and brought it down on the electrical instrument.

Glass crashed and sparks flew. The man fell backward onto the ground. Wires dangled from inside the smashed tubes. The barrel rolled harmlessly away, down the row of other beer barrels.

"Hey! What the hell are you doing?"

Panicked, the man whirled himself around.

"You've broken my television, you cretin!"

The man saw Rudi leaning on his broom high above him. Not knowing which way to run, his legs moved impotently to one side, then to the other. Then the man saw that Rudi was alone.

He began to climb the long wooden ladder toward the loft.

"Get back!" Rudi warned. "You've gotten into enough trouble for one day!"

But the man, with a large square head and dark, dark eyes, kept coming forward.

"My friend has gone for the police!"

But the man climbed to the top of the ladder. He set himself on the loft. Rudi backed away, until his body was against the wooden wall. His hand reached for the door handle, but fumbled. It was too far away. The man was coming closer.

"All right! I warned you!" Rudi set his fists in front of him and lowered his head. He braced his feet. "I'm not afraid of you!"

Rudi had no way of expecting what hit him. A blow that staggered him and broke his jaw, smashed through his upraised fists like iron, and sent him into the dark.

Dimly, he felt sickened. His arms flailed uselessly. It seemed the hard, hefty body was below him. He flailed all the harder, for he felt himself being carried to the edge of the platform. . . .

*   *   *

"Don't speak," Bauer said. "Write. I know it is painful."

The man's back was broken. The jaw was encased in steel wires and plaster. The face was broken, barely discernible underneath the bandages.

"Ten minutes," said the attendant doctor, "no more."

"Did he say anything?" Bauer asked.

175

"N." The patient pointed to the letter on a pad of paper for *Nein*.

"Did he scream, or make any noises?"

"N."

"But when he saw you, he seemed to know his way around the rafters?"

"J." He pointed to the letter on the pad for *Ja*.

"Two meters and a few centimeters in height? Is that correct?"

"J."

"That is what the other laborer said," Steinman said to Bauer, writing all this down.

"A hundred kilos?"

"J."

"And he destroyed the television set before he saw you?"

"J."

"And he wore blue. Slacks and a shirt? Casual?"

"N."

"Not blue?"

"J."

"Not casual?"

"N."

"What then? Pajamas? Institutional wear?"

"J."

"Do you have that, Paul? Institutional wear or pajamas. I want to know every institution in Germany that supplies blue wear. One pocket or two?" he asked the poor man.

There was no response.

"I said, 'one pocket or two?'" Bauer repeated.

Again the man was immobile.

The doctor approached Bauer. Grim faced, he said, "He doesn't know, Inspector, and now you must leave. For the health of this man."

"Yes. Of course, certainly."

Steinman accompanied Bauer out the door. Koenig stood beside the outer corridor.

"I want you to keep watch on the floor," Bauer said to the patrolman. "Discuss with the doctor who is his family and who not, and let no one else into the ward."

Steinman asked, "Do you think he resembles someone, too?"

Bauer shook his head.

"No. The other laborer said that they were not noticed at first. It was only after he smashed the television set, and Rudi shouted down at him, that he became aware of him."

"I don't understand," Steinman said. "What was there about the television set?"

Bauer clapped a hand on Steinman's shoulder.

"Paul," he said kindly, as to a child, "you're too young to remember. There *was* no television before 1945."

*   *   *

He drank from the rain puddle.

Cats crawled among the garbage cans. Spiders dangled on their threads in the dim twilight. Under the massive stone walls, the light faded rapidly.

His shirt sleeves were torn, scratched, and bloodied. The heels of his shoes were broken off. Dirt lined his face, creased it, had worked its way into the corners of his mouth. And he had lost the dynamite.

He stopped. His ears strained. Footsteps were coming down the alley. He threw himself into the doorway of the church, where the shadow obscured him.

The footsteps increased, a man's regular steps over stone.

He pressed himself backward against the door until the wood creaked. An old door, it gave way. He was catapulted backward into the shrine.

He scrambled to his knees. Replacing the door on its hinges, he leaned against it with all his might. The huge shoulders heaved and trembled with muscular fatigue. The footsteps outside went by and retreated down the alley.

He looked into the church. In the front pew, an old woman knelt before the magnificent paintings on the altar, the wrought gold which gracefully ascended to the ceiling, and silver candlesticks which flanked the purple velvet pulpit. He limped into the church proper.

Only the old woman was there, and she was too involved in prayer to pay any attention to anything behind her . . . to notice the big man limping to a small pool in a basin. There the water was cleaner, though warm. It assuaged his thirst. His trembling face received the water gratefully, and the dirt trickled down his arms and hands. He stood thus, exhausted, bent over the font of holy water.

The pool stopped quivering, and he saw his reflection.

"My God!" It was a strangled cry of terror and disbelief.

This face could not be his. Yet it responded to his nerves, his fingers. Altered, deformed, larger and coarser, he felt at his face like a mask that did not fit correctly. And while the old woman knelt before the crucifix, he bit his fingers in anguish, for something had been done to him, some terrible experiment perhaps, and he no longer remembered what it was.

A priest, seeing the disheveled clothes, the dirty hair, decided not to approach. Instead, he went into the luxurious, mahogany privacy of the offertory.

MUNICH:
The Fourteenth Day of Oktoberfest

CHAPTER SIXTEEN

The main gates of Brautnacht Sanitarium opened massively onto a large gravel driveway when Koenig pushed them open.

Spiders hung in the long grass in the sunshine, and far down the row of wooded hills, the twin copper towers of the Frauenkirche just cleared the top of the foliage.

Koenig drove into the yard in his blue and white police mini-car. A number of inmates, wearing blue slacks and shirts, looked up pleasantly at him as he came by.

Koenig noted that the lawn was green and well kept. An ancient stone deer stood amid the tumbled stones of a functioning sculptured fountain. Beneath it, a boy, bound and trussed in leather strapping, lay immobile, staring in hypnotic fascination at the dripping water.

Koenig knocked on the door. The sound echoed down a long hall inside.

Like all the others, Koenig thought wearily. The dozens and dozens of similar institutions his superior, Steinman, had insisted he visit personally, and officially. And with no better result than—

The door opened, closed ever so slightly, and then opened wider. A man with a stern and dignified face stood before Koenig.

"Dr. Kaufmann?" Koenig asked.

The doctor nodded.

"I am here to inquire about any patient whose illness might have been centered around a Nazi obsession," Koenig said.

"You . . . telephoned me before, did you not?"

"Yes. Now I must see your rolls personally. This is formal procedure," Koenig explained.

"Certainly. If you will come back tomorrow, I shall have them organized for you."

"I am supposed to see them this afternoon, Dr. Kaufmann."

"Things are so disorganized at the end of the day," Kaufmann explained.

"I will see them now," Koenig said, a little imperiously.

"Certainly," Kaufmann said.

Koenig entered the long, dark marble hallway and followed Kaufmann into a small office. Kaufmann switched on a light, revealing a jumble of files, transcripts, and medical journals piled high on the desk.

"I told you it was disorganized," Kaufmann said.

Koenig's finger passed down the line of file folders held vertically on the end of the desk. He picked out a folder and opened it. Then he took from his pocket a small pair of spectacles.

Dr. Kaufmann stared with some annoyance at him. Koenig coughed once or twice and began reading down the files. When he was through, he put them back and began on the next set.

"Really, Officer, this will take until midnight if you read every file folder. If you have some suspicion of me, then make it plain."

"No suspicion," Koenig apologized, "but one must be thorough, no?"

Koenig read down the lines of the folder, put it back, and began on the third. Kaufmann crossed his legs. Koenig finished it, and reached for the fourth file.

"Where is September 22?" Koenig asked.

"With the rest, I'm sure."

"No. It doesn't seem to be here," Koenig said. "I'll finish the others, and you see if you can find it for me."

"Good heavens, Officer," Kaufmann said, rising. "I must protest. I have been a licensed physician for thirty-three years and I have never been subjected to such official stupidity. Why didn't you let us know in advance? We would have had all the files in order, complete, and ready for you. Certainly your superiors are accustomed to treating the public with greater respect."

Koenig looked up, flustered.

"My superiors," Koenig said, regaining his composure, "are accustomed to receiving greater obedience from the general public. Now please find me the missing week."

Kaufmann wiped a nervous hand across his mouth.

"I don't have it," he said.

"You don't have it?"

"I spilled ink all over it and it is being recopied."

"Where is it now?"

"In the basement," Kaufmann said, "where my wife—my nurse —does her bookkeeping."

"Well, hurry, please. It's getting late."

Kaufmann edged away, hesitantly, and left the room. At length, Koenig heard whispering in the hall which cut short at the door. Kaufmann and his wife, a small, tautly smiling woman, entered. In her hand was a file folder.

Koenig took the folder from her and carefully examined it.

181

"Where's Hass?" Koenig said.

"Who?"

"William Hass. The daily record for William Hass ends September 22." Koenig turned the paper over. "There's nothing else." He looked up.

Kaufmann and the woman said nothing, clearing their throats, waiting for the other to speak.

"No meals, no waking hours, no sleeping time—nothing."

Kaufmann and his wife again said nothing. The wife smiled nervously.

"Well," she said. "He's asleep."

"Asleep? For two weeks?"

"No. Of course not." She laughed. "Ah—drug therapy," she said, "and so the usual entries are not made—"

"Drugs?" Koenig asked, closing the folder.

"No," Kaufmann said. "No drugs. We don't give drugs. It's just that he has been in isolated treatment—"

"You are not licensed to administer drugs, are you, Dr. Kaufmann?"

"We give no drugs here."

"But your wife just said—"

"You fool!" Kaufmann suddenly screamed, standing up. He turned on his wife, backing away as though she were something unclean. "You gross idiot! What's this about drugs? He would never have known—I would have thought of something!"

Koenig stood, confused.

"What's going on here?" Koenig said.

The woman suddenly leaned forward.

"He escaped," she said. "Because of the pictures. I told my husband it was no good, but he has a stubborn head. Remember, I told you this of my own account."

"Yes, thank you," Koenig said. "But what, really, are you talking about? If you gave him drugs and are not licensed—"

"We didn't give him drugs, idiot!" roared Kaufmann.

Koenig frowned.

"Well, well, Kaufmann. Hunt a pheasant and flush a quail. I come here looking for a Nazi killer and I find you have been keeping improper records, lying to me, and insulting me."

The livid, twitching face of Dr. Kaufmann met his glance. Koenig slowly removed his spectacles.

"Let's just see what this patient Hass has to say about all this, shall we?"

The doctor hit the side of his leg in disbelieving anger.

"He's not here," the nurse said. "That's what I've been trying to tell you."

Dr. Kaufmann looked out the window, the bars already throwing those ominous black stripes across his face. Koenig sat down, perplexed.

"I must call headquarters. Where is your phone?"

Steinman received the call. Wearily, he listened to the slow-speaking, monotonous voice at the other end. Steinman yawned. Then he caught his yawn and listened closely.

"What color is their uniform?"

"I don't know, sir."

"Ask them!"

"Yes, sir."

Koenig put a hand over the receiver.

"What color are your uniforms?" Koenig asked.

"Blue," said the nurse.

"Blue," Koenig repeated into the receiver.

Kaufmann shot his wife a look.

"Bring them in," Steinman said.

"They can't fit into the car," Koenig protested. "I have only the 350. If you would issue the 450s to the patrolmen—"

"Bring them in, Koenig!"

"Yes, sir."

Steinman hung up. Koenig turned to the doctor and his wife,

who sat looking in opposite directions from each other, the nurse attempting a nervous smile at Koenig.

"I explained to my superior that the car is too small, but he insists on seeing you both right away. So, we must go, now."

The nurse rose, protesting.

"Those are my orders," Koenig said. "I have nothing to do with it."

In the Justice Building, Steinman sat at his desk, his hand resting on the telephone receiver which he had just hung up. A soft beacon of light fell through the frosted glass doors of the interrogation room down the hall. Thinking a moment, Steinman stood and walked quickly down the hall, toward the closed doors.

Inside, a pimply youth sat surly on a bench and looked down at the floor. A young girl stood screaming over him, while several uniformed police looked on for a reaction from him.

"Clear the room," Steinman said, and bounded up the marble stairs, past the statuary, the paintings of the old generals, and came quickly onto the upper floor. There, breathing heavily, he knocked on the dark wooden door of the conference room.

"Who is it?" came Bauer's voice.

"Steinman, sir."

"Come in, Paul."

Steinman opened the door and entered, closing it carefully behind him. At the end of the huge table sat his superior, weary against the darkening window, in the twilight. In his hand were photographs at least two decades old, plus police reports from all the neighboring towns.

At the other end of the table, just returned from Bonn, sat Madeline Kress, bent over the reports and files from local jails, precincts and prisons throughout southern Germany. Between them lay a mound of discarded documents and photographs.

Steinman dared to beckon delicately to Bauer. Bauer raised

an eyebrow and, pulling himself out of his chair, came quickly across the room until he was beside Steinman.

"I think we have a break," Steinman said.

*   *   *

Bauer looked with satisfaction at the pale face of Dr. Kaufmann. Not that such a face fills one with respect. Far from it. But the Inspector knew that such faces breed mistakes and minor guilts. There was good possibility that the night might yield, for the first time, some tangible result into the investigation.

"Close the windows, Paul," Bauer said. "Make it dark in here."

Dr. Kaufmann stood perspiring under a circle of light in the interrogation room. As Steinman pulled the blinds closed, the circle of light grew more intense.

The Colonel walked into the room. He proceeded to the cabinets and drawers of files which had been lifted in their entirety from the Brautnacht Sanitarium. Colonel Schuckert nodded to Bauer to begin.

"Wait, gentlemen," Kaufmann said with a nervous laugh. "There aren't enough chairs . . ."

"Don't worry, Kaufmann," the Chief Inspector said. "It is as we like it."

Bauer stood against the table, leaning backward a little, so that the light shone off his chest. A short distance in front of him, sitting on the one chair in the room, was the doctor.

Madeline Kress and Steinman entered. Steinman closed the door quietly, and all sounds of the passers-by in the hall faded.

"You had an incomplete entry," Bauer began.

Kaufmann, at first confused because he had expected the Colonel, attired in Army uniform, to lead the questioning, now looked at Bauer. Colonel Schuckert ignored the doctor altogether, and was busy paging through the files in the drawers heaped on a table under the windows.

"Well, that is to say—" Kaufmann said.

"And his name is Hass."

"Well, yes. Hass."

The doctor's hands were folded. In the warm room his glasses were getting fogged.

"Hass," Bauer said, demanding some sort of answer.

"William Hass," Kaufmann said.

"Jew?"

"Circumcised. Yes."

Kaufmann began to resent the tone in which he was being addressed. After all, he was not a suspect.

"Where did you get him?"

"I beg your pardon?"

Bauer leaned forward. Rather impolitely close, Kaufmann thought.

"Where did William Hass come from?" Bauer demanded.

"One of those concentration camps."

"Which one?"

"Auschwitz, I believe."

"You believe?"

"It was Auschwitz."

Bauer paused.

"That long ago, Kaufmann?"

"Yes." Kaufmann wiped his face. "It was right after the war. A man named Berger—another inmate of Auschwitz—brought him to us."

Colonel Schuckert looked up from the files.

"It says in this report by Berger that after the Russians liberated Auschwitz, he and William Hass escaped, and walked across Poland to Munich."

Madeline's eyes narrowed in remembrance.

"Many of us were smuggled out of Auschwitz—by the Jewish underground group known as Brichah."

"Smuggled? Escaped?" Bauer was totally confused. "I don't understand. If the war was over, and they were liberated . . . ?"

Madeline's laughter cut his words short.

"For you, the war was over, Inspector. But not for us. The seeds Germany sowed fell on fertile ground. You showed the world how simple the matter of getting rid of Jews could be. After the liberation, thousands of Jewish refugees were still being bullied and murdered, by Poles, Russians, Romanians—you name it. Wherever we turned, we found hatred."

During her speech, Bauer's eyes remained steadfastly fixed on Dr. Kaufmann.

"All right, Kaufmann, continue. After Hass and Berger got to Munich, then what happened?"

"I told you," Kaufmann said. "Berger brought him to Brautnacht, and left him in our care. Hass was too ill to continue on the journey. In fact, he was at death's door."

"I see," Bauer said. "And you took him in as an act of simple charity?"

"No, I—" Kaufmann began sweating again. "That is, Berger left some jewels . . . to pay for his treatments."

"Jewels?"

"Some baubles. They didn't amount to very much."

"Diamonds?"

"Yes."

"And where did Berger, a victim of Auschwitz, come by these diamonds?" There was clearly an edge of doubt in Bauer's tone.

"He had them, I tell you," Kaufmann insisted. "Throughout his incarceration, he had them."

"And they were never discovered?"

"No. He told me that he secreted them . . . in various orifices in his body."

During the long pause which followed, only the ticking of the wall clock could be heard.

At length Bauer continued.

"And during all these years, the only support you got for William Hass were those diamonds?"

Kaufmann's eyes sought the floor.

"No," he said, in a soft whisper.

"Speak up!" Colonel Schuckert prodded.

"From time to time we receive a money draft, drawn on the Israel National Bank."

"From Berger?" demanded Bauer.

"Yes," Kaufmann snapped. "And we have always acknowledged receipt of his drafts, and have additionally rendered to him full reports on the precise progress of the patient's health." Kaufmann waved a hand toward the files. "Look for yourself, it is a matter of record."

Bauer could only shake his head, and continue to gaze at Kaufmann's moist, feverish face glistening beneath the harsh light.

"There are other documents in this file," Colonel Schuckert said, reading from a sheaf of invoices, "that speak of further reimbursements you received from the German government as part of the Reparations Act, Dr. Kaufmann?"

"A stipend." Kaufmann shrugged.

"I see," Bauer said. "You were collecting from both ends?"

Kaufmann did not answer. Though he still retained a semblance of his former composure, he kept his eyes firmly glued to a spot on the floor.

It was Madeline who spoke next.

"After the war, there *was* confusion. But later—" Madeline softly sought her words with care. "There were Jewish agencies. They would certainly have helped him."

"Perhaps," Kaufmann said distastefully. "But they didn't come to Brautnacht."

"Why not?"

"How should I know? They didn't know about Brautnacht, I guess."

"And you didn't bother to tell them," Madeline said, "for fear of losing your 'stipends'?"

"Or," Bauer added, "to report his escape for the same reason, eh, Kaufmann?"

There was a moment of silence, as Kaufmann's eyes sought Madeline's in a long, accusatory stare.

"What about Berger?" Kaufmann softly asked. "He knew about William Hass. Why did he not consult with your Jewish agencies?"

Kaufmann allowed his words to sink in fully.

"I'll tell you why," he continued. "Because it was no use. Because William Hass had ceased to be. And Berger knew it."

Bauer sat on the edge of the table. His face was inches from Kaufmann's.

"Go on, Kaufmann, tell us. What was William Hass like?"

"A stone."

"Let us be more precise," Colonel Schuckert said from the far end of the room.

"A rock, a brick. He felt nothing, said nothing, reacted to nothing."

"All that time?" Bauer asked.

"I repeat, for twenty-eight years he lived in a hole of his own making. Nothing we did could arouse him—loud noises, electric stimuli, bright colors, tests of all kinds—nothing. You might as well speak to a wall."

"But he was aware," Bauer said, "of things that went on around him?"

Kaufmann broke his dignified pose. He became exasperated.

"No! Don't you understand that? He did not exist! He was dead! Catatonic amnesia. Except for the basic bodily functions, he *was* not."

"I find that difficult to believe," the Chief Inspector muttered. "Not to know anything, anything at all, for so long a period of time."

There was silence. Bauer looked toward Madeline. Madeline did not know whether to believe it or not. In the respite, Kaufmann mopped his forehead and replaced the handkerchief in his breast pocket.

"And he never improved?" Bauer asked.

"Never improved."

"Then what brought him out of it?"

Colonel Schuckert stepped forward into the edge of light. A file folder containing a dossier on William Hass and a selection of photographs were in his arms. He extracted the photographs, bent over, and showed them to Kaufmann.

"These were therapy?" the Colonel asked.

"Yes," Kaufmann said rather archly. "We hoped to jog his memory."

"You did your job well."

In Schuckert's hands were pictures of Jews mounted against wooden fences, impaled there by knives, and they sagged downward, their striped pajama suits tearing from the weight of their own bodies. Soft, intellectual faces peered out nearsightedly through the barbed wire, unable to comprehend who was taking their picture, or why. Skeletons with hair opened their mouths toward the heavens, as guards heaved them one by one onto dusty trucks.

"Where did you get those pictures?" Madeline asked. She and Steinman had come forward to examine the photographs.

"I had them duplicated from an American source. For scientific purposes."

Bauer turned to hand the photographs back to Colonel Schuckert, but the Colonel was engrossed in the dossier on William Hass. His face was grim. When finally he spoke, his voice was hollow, stripped of emotion, and seeming to taste the bitterness of each word.

"Berger says here that William Hass was an architect before the war. Some of his buildings are still standing in Germany. He was one of the first we put away. Right here, outside Munich. Dachau—he and his family. A wife, Ilse, and their child, Anna, aged seven. The wife and child were killed at Dachau—and he was sent to Auschwitz . . ."

Except for Kaufmann, who sat twitching nervously, each person in the room remained motionless during the recital.

It was Bauer who finally broke the silence.

"And after twenty-eight years of nothingness, it was these pictures that caused him to wake up?"

"Who knows?" Kaufmann shrugged. "The mechanism of amnesia is very mysterious."

"It seems bizarre to me," Bauer said.

"Bizarre? To you?" Madeline laughed bitterly. "How do you think *he* feels? To him it is still 1945. And he's just escaped from Auschwitz!"

*   *   *

Leaving the interrogation room, Bauer, Madeline, and Colonel Schuckert descended the long staircase in silence—their hands caressing the white marble railing worn smooth by decades of other hands. At the foot of the stairs, carrying a briefcase under his arm, District Attorney Hugo Flanck climbed to meet them.

Schuckert's eyes narrowed instinctively. He kept his hawk-like gaze on Flanck as they approached each other. There was an impasse.

Flanck smiled.

"A gift for you, Inspector," he said.

He handed Bauer a long white envelope. Bauer opened it and removed a number of long, legal-sized sheets of paper.

"All quite official," Flanck said. "One from the Ministry of the Interior and the other from Bonn. Authorizing me to relieve you. As of this moment, I am personally in charge."

Bauer watched the District Attorney, expressionless. Colonel Schuckert took two steps down, until he was directly in front of Flanck.

Frank De Felitta

"He is not a criminal, Flanck," the Colonel said. "He is not responsible for what he is doing. He must not be killed, if that is humanly possible. You understand, Flanck!"

Flanck's eyes sparkled in something like merriment.

"Your suggestion," he said, "shall receive my consideration."

Colonel Schuckert moved closer to Flanck, until the District Attorney was aware of the man's bulk looming over him. The Colonel's eyes were ablaze. He put a finger under Flanck's nose.

"It is a point of German honor," he whispered hoarsely. "If you harm this man, the whole world will know you! You understand me, Flanck!"

The smile on Flanck's face froze. Then he stepped back again and revived the smile. He nodded toward the Colonel and to Bauer. Upon Madeline he fixed a dark and ironic expression. He pushed his way through them and continued up the stairway.

Bauer's face was tight. He slowly put the legal-sized documents into his pocket. But his eyes shone with a black fire.

Continuing down the stairway, Madeline, Bauer, and the Colonel stayed close together. A bond had formed between them. Unspoken, yet known to each. Incredibly, purposely, none had bothered to mention to the new man in charge of the case the fact of Kaufmann's confession, and the more astounding knowledge that they had positively identified the killer.

CHAPTER SEVENTEEN

"You have fallen into a void," Bauer said. "It's at the bottom of a well. You are nothing. You see nothing. You hear nothing. Life does not exist for you. Your senses present no evidence of an external world. Not even of the darkness are you aware.

"Then one day it wears off. Inexplicably, mysteriously the darkness peels away, layer by layer. Like a dreamer slowly waking, you ascend from the depths of a well, and you see in front of you a photograph of Jews in the compound—"

"With whom you spoke only yesterday," Madeline said.

Madeline and Bauer walked down the brightly lit streets of Munich. Shining traffic swirled on the boulevards. Shoppers crowded the concrete department stores for winter fashions. Welcome banners hung loosely in the cold breeze over the intersections.

"The leering face of Dr. Kaufmann," Bauer said, "watches your every reaction."

"You are still in a concentration camp," Madeline said. "You have been part of an experiment, which has caused you to pass out for a moment, but you are now revived."

Together they walked across a street, passing alongside a black iron railing, walking toward the parks and away from the Hall of Justice and its bright lights.

"You are frightened, because you cannot recognize where you are—" Bauer said.

"It is because they have tampered with your mind."

"You know only that Nazis are everywhere, and you must escape."

Foliage of red and yellow in the trees overhead darkened now as the lights of the Hall of Justice receded, and leaves dropped one by one, drifting downward in slants on the breeze, across their path.

"But surely the architecture is changed," Bauer said. "It is peacetime. People are celebrating a festival. Won't he see that, sooner or later?"

"How could you convince a man that twenty-eight years have passed without his knowing it? How could you explain it? Could *you* believe it?"

"But his appearance? His hair, his face, the lines of age . . ."

"The result of experiments."

Droplets of vapor hung in vague halos around the globe lights strung through the park. It displeased Bauer, for it reminded him of the night on which the janitor was found.

"There's another thing, Inspector, which you must remember."

Madeline walked beside him, a kerchief over her head to keep away the chill. Her hands in her pockets, she looked down at the colored leaves tamped onto the path through the park.

"Have you forgotten how enthusiastically the German people marched behind the Führer? How willingly they smashed the

shops of Jews all over the Reich? How is he to know that outside the concentration camp, the Germans are *not* continuing
that celebration?"

Couples walked slowly down the darkening paths, or sat on
benches together as Madeline and Bauer passed.

"But you see, Miss Kress," Bauer said. "All this—until the
edge of town—was bombed. Munich was nearly in rubble. I,
myself, helped lay the railroad tracks which we used to trans-
port all the debris to the outskirts of town. People were starving
here."

Madeline said nothing as they turned a corner and once more
walked under the bright lights of Munich's prosperous avenues.

"Possibly, Inspector Bauer," Madeline said at last, "but how is
he to know that?"

"Of course, you're right."

As he had feared, the droplets of night vapor had turned to
a light mist. Already wisps of cloud floated about the rococo
columns under which they passed. It gave the Inspector an uncomfortable feeling.

Madeline walked silently alongside him. As they approached
the area of the Wittelsbach bridge, the old town looming over
them and the cobblestones gleaming now in the precipitation,
her eyes took on a fearful curiosity.

Bauer noticed the fear which had entered her eyes.

"Excuse me," he said lightly, "but the French must be sabotag-
ing our Oktoberfest by sending rain. Will you wait here under
the awning and not leave me?"

Madeline nodded. The Inspector left her a brief moment,
and, looking both ways, darted quickly over the shining rails in
the road to a small, bright shop, in an old wall of shops under
striped awnings.

"An umbrella," he said. "Quickly, please."

"Right behind you, sir."

"Excuse me? Oh, yes. Good heavens. Twenty marks?"

"Anything less will dissolve in the rain."

"I doubt it. Here. Hurry, please."

Under the awning, across the traffic which obscured her from time to time, Madeline appeared to the Inspector extraordinarily small and fragile. Gone was the toughness of the conference rooms, the darting mind of the accusations. As she stood there, her hands held together in front of her, waiting patiently for his return, he was moved to try to protect her.

The Inspector ran quickly back over the road, slipping a little on the wet streetcar rails embedded in the stones.

"After the rain," he said, "it will be winter. It rains for a week or so, and then it gets very cold. The fields turn to brown. The trees are bare. And the snows creep day by day down the Alps until the hills all around Munich are covered with snow. That is the best time."

Madeline looked at him strangely.

"I know, Inspector," she said. "I remember."

Embarrassed, the Inspector was silent a moment. Then he saw the fear once again in her eyes.

"Would you like to go back?"

She shook her head.

"No," she said. "I asked you to take me here. Only it frightens me, now, after all these years."

In front of them was the alley of the old town, over which balconies leaned out, lined with boxes of red flowers. The cobbled roads fed into the alley, finally merging into one road to cross the Isar by the Wittelsbach bridge. The rain now pattered down on the umbrella which Bauer held over their heads. It was in this neighborhood that Madeline had grown up.

"Nothing has changed," she said.

Bauer accompanied her to a row of shops which turned down the alley. The street was deserted, only the sound of dripping water making a noise in the night. The walls, with their plaster broken, the wooden beams in rows supporting the roofs, seemed so familiar to her, as though, if pressed, she could have named each and every house, the family, and the fate of each.

"Would you mind—?" Madeline asked. "I would like to be alone here again. Just for a minute."

"I'm not sure that would be wise. We are near the construction site where the janitor—"

"Only a minute, Inspector. I beg you."

Bauer handed her the umbrella reluctantly.

"I shall keep out of sight," he said.

While Bauer leaned uncomfortably back against the wall, under the uncertain shelter of a wooden balcony over his head, the drizzle out in front of him, Madeline walked under the umbrella down the lane. The buildings leaned in on her, old stone buildings, farmhouses once, and lofts converted to living rooms, facing the stone embankments of the dark Isar rumbling below her.

The figurines carved upon the bridge looked at her as she passed by. Elegant, graceful, they seemed ethereal in the rain mist and half light of the distant street lamps, writhing and twisting in a macabre dance in stone. The pavement glistened under her feet. The rain water circled down around the lampposts and ran to meet her footsteps.

"Oh, Mutti!" Madeline said. "Mutti!"

The trees blew with force as a sudden breeze stirred up the water on the roofs. Boats on the river bobbed on the black water. Water grasses waved violently under the stones. A wagon stood, its rotting slats glistening oddly in the off-yellow light of the obscured street lamps.

From where Bauer stood, he watched Madeline walking carelessly into the dark lanes. He moved to follow her, adjusting his collar around his neck.

"Where is St. Boniface?"

Startled, Bauer turned suddenly. An old woman, her kerchief tied around her head, looked up slyly at him.

197

"Do you know where St. Boniface is, sir?"

"Excuse me. I—I—"

"But surely you must know where it is. I am looking for it. I—have lost my way."

Bauer turned away. Madeline was already out of sight.

"Please," he said. "Excuse me—"

But she stood in front of him. Bauer noticed that she was partially blind. That was why she looked at him out of the corner of her eyes. It gave her that peculiar, sly look.

"But you *do* know where it is?" she insisted.

"Down this road," Bauer pointed. "And to the left. You will not miss it."

The old woman turned laboriously around to follow Bauer's pointing finger.

"Thank you, young man. Thank you. I am most grateful."

But Bauer had left, and was walking quickly through the rain, holding his collar tight around his neck.

Everywhere the streets were deserted. Down the river the Braunauer bridge spanned darkly the rapidly coursing water. The railroad passed over that bridge. Bauer looked down the long line of tracks that led to a cluster of buildings into an area of lights which were the central train station.

"Madeline!" he called softly.

The rain answered him.

"Madeline!"

Madeline, out of earshot, looked down into the rushing water, where no depth could be seen. The railing was now so much smaller. The houses, too, were smaller. But it smelled the same. The smell of the air, the cold of the rain, circulated freely, enticingly through her bones and revived ancient memories—memories of a person she had long thought had been turned to stone.

She heard footsteps coming slowly over the bridge.

Here she had dropped rocks into the river. Here she had once tied banners onto the lampposts. Here the old man with one leg had threatened her for picking his flowers. Here—

The footsteps came regularly, shoe leather on wet stone.

Madeline turned. But it was not the Inspector.

"Good evening," a male voice said. "Are you lost?"

Madeline shook her head. She brushed her cheeks with her hand, which felt warm against the cold air.

"You seemed confused," the voice said. "Or I would not have stopped."

The silhouetted form came a step closer, into the muted light of a distant lamppost. It was a boy, an adolescent, with a peaked cap over his head. The rain ran freely onto his jacket and down the leather strap of the pouch he was carrying. It was a pouch full of bicycle tools, gleaming up from under the towel he had thrown over them.

"No," Madeline said. "But I—"

"Downtown Munich is that way." The boy pointed. "Giesing that way."

Perhaps sixteen, his face was still not in the habit of being shaved. Dark curls framed his face wetly under the black corduroy cap.

"Do you live here?" Madeline asked.

"Beyond those boats."

"It is late for you?"

"I have been to the fairgrounds."

"Tell me—"

"Yes?"

"Do you know the name Eisenberg?"

"No."

"Katie and Samuel Eisenberg. They were jewelers and lived here."

"No. I don't know Eisenberg."

"Rudolfs—Hilda and Wolf Rudolfs? And Margarite—? She's— Oh, no—she is not your age."

The boy shook his head, not understanding.

"Don't you know Margarite? She was a redhead?"

"I don't know them. I'm sorry," he said.

"But she was so pretty."

"Are you from America?" the boy asked.

"What? No. No."

"Canada, then," he said. "Sometimes I see Canadians come here. From Toronto. They also ask about people. But I don't know many of them."

"Yes, but—" Madeline said, confused. "Everything else is the same."

"My father is president of the jeweler's guild. He knows all the families here. He was fire warden during the war."

"No, no—"

"It's all right. Most people who come here looking, talk to him. He knows what happened to them."

Madeline heard footsteps approaching rapidly again. A man's heavy footsteps, nearly running.

"Madeline!" Inspector Bauer called.

Madeline and the boy looked at Bauer, wilted and wetly shining, approaching them rapidly. His hair glistened from the rain. He breathed heavily. His coat was soaked through.

"You worried me," he confessed. "I lost sight of you."

"It's all right, Inspector," Madeline said. All at once reality had penetrated her again. In despair, she felt now even the memories of the past had turned to black vapor and escaped, like the soul at the moment of death. The Isar bubbled and fumed downstream, an empty sound now, holding no meaning for her but the steady, indifferent passage of time. The stone houses which dripped seemed to have no meaning beyond themselves. German houses in a Bavarian side street, dripping, dripping with the remnants of a cloudburst, their secrets, and who they were meant for, no longer clear to Madeline.

"It's all right," she said. "Quite all right."

The rain beat down, harder.

"Do you want some help?" said the boy. "My father can get a cab."

"That won't be necessary," Bauer said.

Not trusting the Inspector, the boy asked again, "Can I help you, miss?"

But Madeline stirred herself from the stone rail, and joined the Inspector. Together the Inspector, drenched in his dark clothes, and the woman turned their backs on the boy and walked slowly up and over the Wittelsbach bridge, toward Munich's center.

The boy watched them go, oddly stirred. He wondered if he should tell his father. Then he, too, went away in the rain, the leather pouch of bicycle tools slapping wetly against his leg. He disappeared, and the rain beat insistently on the yellow lights and stone walls of the old town.

*   *   *

In the apartment where Bauer lived, however, the light was not so soft. A harsh white emanated from the kitchen where Madeline took off her coat, then her shoes. Her hair was disheveled. She took a small kettle from the wall and filled it with water. She put it upon the stove and seemed not to know that the Inspector was still in the next room. He stood there, hat in hand, watching her in the kitchen, seeming to weigh his thoughts, and hesitant to speak.

"There is a new synagogue in Munich," he said finally. "I could take you there."

"No. No. I don't want to see it."

"No?"

"I never want to see anything here again. It is dead. I am dead. Everything died in the war."

Bauer turned away from her and gazed out the window.

Flashes of light, brought by sheets of falling rain water, swept across the black windows.

"I am going home," Madeline said. "I can't stay here any more."

Madeline only looked down on the water in the kettle. Under the broad white light her face looked more lined, wearier, than it had before. As though the part of her that was still child had died.

The Inspector took one step closer to her.

"Then Flanck shall have him killed."

"Or he will kill himself. Often they did that."

Madeline looked up and saw Bauer's silhouette across the room, and behind him the alternating black and white of the storm-illumined window. Bauer's form was distinct, poised; he did not know whether to remain or approach.

"You must not leave," Bauer said, his soft voice filled with a strange note of urgency. "You are essential."

Then he saw her eyes.

Deep gray, deep as the night which threw its storm against his windows. Without mercy, with darkness, they looked on him with a coldness he had rarely seen.

"How you judge us . . ." he said.

Madeline said nothing, only looked at him.

"I have come to care so much what you think of us . . . of me . . ." the Inspector continued. "But it is no good. You have no capacity to care for us."

Madeline shook her head, as though ridding herself of hearing him.

"You are filled with a hatred which guides you through life," he said softly.

"Don't, Inspector. I warn you not to do this."

"And you have no compassion."

Madeline backed away. She kept her eyes on the bubbles of air liberated from the kettle. She sensed that the Inspector was watching her intently. Her fear of him rose to the surface again.

"You want compassion?" she said. "I can give you only hate."

"Hate? Do you know what that is?"

"No one better than I."

"No. You can hate only a person that you know."

"I hate Germans," she said.

"An abstraction!" he said. "Look beneath, and you'll find humans, with faults and weaknesses."

"Yes. More than anything. Faults . . . and weaknesses."

The Inspector had approached until he fairly stood over her.

"How can you hate weakness?" he said. "Tell me. I was weak. Can you hate me for it?"

"Yes, you were the worst," she said. "There were the death dealers, the perverted doctors and the bureaucrats, the nurses—the guards—the crematorium stokers. They were bad. But—you—fine, decent, *weak* people, who never asked, who shut out the sight and pretended it didn't exist . . ."

"Very well," Bauer shouted. "Go back to Yad Vashem! Wrap yourself in your hatreds there! Feed yourself on them till you are glutted with hatred! Then maybe you will be as sick and fanatical as the Nazis!"

He grabbed her arm as she turned away from him.

"Do not touch me, Inspector Bauer!"

"You will listen to me, Madeline! You will know that I saw the Jews from a train, piling into Auschwitz! I saw them going under the barbed wire! I saw them trudging through the snow! And I knew where they were going—though I pretended I didn't—I *knew*— We all knew—" The Inspector's voice was trembling. He realized he was trying to keep from weeping in front of her. "We all knew—" he repeated. "And never cared," he said in a softer voice. "Because what were Jews? Who were the Jews to us? We were willing to be carried by the tide of insanity—because we feared—more than we cared."

The Inspector had taken out a cigarette. The trembling fingers fumbled with the lighter.

"It was only after the war," he said, very softly. "We realized we'd killed ourselves. We were none of us alive after that. I have never been alive since then."

"Nor I!" Madeline cried hoarsely. "Nor I."

"No." The Inspector understood. "Nor you."

Madeline began to weep, holding her face away from the Inspector, ashamed in front of him.

"Because we were none of us giants," the Inspector said, as he stood without moving. Behind them, the storm which flashed against the window revealed them both, facing in opposite directions, listening to each other, held in an incommunicable bond.

"No," he murmured. "It's much too late. Much too late. And yet"—he turned softly—"we might have been friends. We are the same kind of people."

Hat in hand, the Inspector went to the door and opened it.

"If you still wish, I will have a car for you in the morning," he said, putting on his hat. He left the umbrella for her.

The door closed.

Madeline wiped her eyes with the back of her hand. Through the wriggling trains of water coursing down the glass pane she saw the Inspector walking quickly out into the night rain.

MUNICH:
The Fifteenth Day of Oktoberfest

CHAPTER EIGHTEEN

The rain had ceased. The skies opened into a sunburst, which revealed two rainbows. A weird, purplish sky.

Bauer walked, hands behind his back, through the fairgrounds. He checked the posts of his patrolmen. Each of them nodded back to his informal acknowledgment.

He approached one, the mud pulling off the soles of his shiny shoes.

"The cleaver killer," Bauer said, almost conversationally. "He has illusions of being a Nazi slayer. Anything reminiscent of the concentration camps—however remote—guard it."

Startled, the patrolman nodded.

"Guard it well," Bauer said. "He must be taken alive."

Bauer walked slowly through his self-appointed rounds, keeping an eye open for his patrolmen. To the next, he added, "You may receive orders somewhat different from mine. But unless you hear from me personally, you will disregard them."

The next patrolman saluted, and the next, as Bauer walked on through the milling crowd.

He walked through the green but wet grass, his black shoes hopelessly soiled. He caught the eye of Steinman and, when Steinman came over, told him the same.

"Flanck's orders are different," Steinman said.

"The hell with Flanck," Bauer said.

*　　*　　*

The voices rose into a shout. The martial drums beat. Throngs of the populace lined the streets of Munich. The police held back the lines. Up the cobblestones they came, up through the old town, under the arches and flowers and banners over the wrought-iron balconies.

The beer wagons rolled by. In blue and silver fringe, the white horses leaned into their harnesses and pulled wagons laden with kegs. Anheuser, Heineken embossed on the side. A fat driver, he with the largest mustache of all, waved, first to one side of the crowd and then to the other.

Then came the bands. Black-hatted, black-coated, or dressed in scarlets of the provinces, they tooted their way up the streets. The crowd pelted them with flowers. Dogs leaped and barked.

All the while the clouds grew darker and darker, for the twilight was fading fast and night was coming in. The lights overhead turned on and turned the faces below to weirder and weirder shades of flesh, red, then green, and then yellow.

The dancers followed. The old women in Bavarian black, and from Franconia, and Holsteiners, holding their handkerchiefs in their hands, sedately coming up the walk. Now and then the men came out and danced with them, sidestepping toward the Meadow at the outskirts of town.

The Oktoberfest was coming to its end. Fifteen days of unrelenting celebration now culminated in this, the last night of the floats.

The craftsmen came, the cobblers, wearing black aprons with pouches, marching in step and holding up their hammers for the crowds. Then the butchers, the slaughterers, red-faced and florid in their rubber aprons—grimly holding pigs on poles, heavy pigs that swung as the butchers carried them onward to the Meadow.

A cheer rose from the crowds.

The King and Queen of Beer, to thunderous applause, waved from a throne of flowers, kissing and drinking beer.

Behind them, the awesome float of the city of Munich rolled on, seven huge breweries on a mountain landscape, and the costumed women in the motions of working the fields.

The town of Bad Tölz—in blacks and greens, and a mock cow and bull on the front. Spinning—swirling in a phantasmagoria of colored chrysanthemums, and a girl gaily riding a horse bareback. And then, up out of the old and painted stone arches which spanned the broken stone roads, came the lumbering, festooned wagons of Dachau—

The wagons passed slowly. A driver, inebriated, slipped at the reins, laughing at himself, and a child ran up to retrieve the reins for him.

Hass emerged from a rubble of broken bottles.

Banners, flower stems, newspapers, paper holdings for sausages, cellophane, plastics, sticks for corn and fish wrappings slipped under his feet. He stood in the shadow where it was already cold and night. He dimly saw the crowd roaring and hooting.

A wagon of forms which was a silhouette against the last bit of light turned the corner. Glittering, blue and gold, under the artificial lights, were the clear Gothic letters which spelled— Dachau.

Hass's eyes quickened. They dilated to a deep, dark black.

But no black void, no hole could ever come again to cover him up. His knuckles whitened and they pressed against his eyes.

"Ilse!"

The Dachau wagon rumbled slowly up toward the road which wound past the fairgrounds. There the crowd was enjoying its last hours, the patrolmen watching over them, and the farmers gathering up their bundles and their wagons.

"Ilse! Anna!"

The floats were rolling toward home. Up over the arc of the hill the horses pulled them, toward the sheds and garages, for the dismantling and the rebuilding for the next year.

Hass moved away from the wall, running low through the shadows into the coming night.

*   *   *

The Oktoberfest was all but over. Tomorrow, the sixteenth day, the day of the "diehards," would bring down the final curtain. The municipality could then begin to count its healthy profits. Throughout the day, trains would be full and flowing with departing Germans and foreigners. The airport would be jammed, and, finally, the hotels could sigh with relief.

The beer pavilions, still full and surging, would stand empty, white as ghosts in the twilight, waiting to be taken down. The expositions would be closed and locked, and night watchmen would patrol the long, empty corridors inside.

But tonight, the fifteenth night of the Oktoberfest, Munich was still held fast in the heady grip of beer, laughter, and song.

In the countryside, the empty trees stood forlorn. The landscape was bare and brown, sodden with the result of last night's rain. In the first darkness of the night, the Alps were only a presence, breathing cool air down from the heights.

The crickets lay low. Bullfrogs embedded themselves in the mud, away from the foraging cows. Pieces of machinery from the farms made their laborious way back to their slanted wooden sheds. From time to time the headlights of a passing automobile cut through the darkened air. A vapor had begun to rise again, a field mist, a wet cloud knee high, and the marsh grasses bent downward with the weight of the water on their stems.

Down the highway, the wagon moved slowly. The old man at the reins was slumped over, snoring lightly, and hiccuping. The white horses pulled the flower-strewn buckboards up the long hill. The old man tapped the horses on the side with the reins, but it made no difference. Slowly, slowly, the wagon made its way up the long, endless hill toward Dachau.

A woman in the back slept soundly, lying on a jacket of one of the three men leaning backward against the empty kegs. A metal stein rolled with the bumps of the wagon, for the hand that was holding it had uncurled in sleep. The old man up front again tapped the reins.

Mosquitoes came out of the fog to nip him above the green knee socks. He wore a green and black Alpine suit. Badges of his beer-drinking prowess dangled from his coat.

Down through the marsh the wagon rolled. The trees passed in silhouette. The fog obscured their topmost branches. The shrubs, like sentries, stiff and unbending, passed by. The weeds rustled.

A horse snorted.

"Easy now," the old man muttered, and tapped the reins against their sides.

The night was quiet, so that from the weeds he heard a heavy, broken breathing. He stopped the wagon.

"Hallo there. Are you all right?"

He squinted out into the darkness.

"What is it? You have trouble?"

The horses neighed impatiently.

He tied the reins down at the side of the driver's bench. He turned and weaved uncertainly toward the weed bank, where a form had appeared in the mud.

The ground teetered and rose, drunkenly, feeling for him. The old man was falling in spite of himself. He giggled.

"I hope you're better off than I—"

The form took him and held him. It took him by the head.

The sleepers snored.

The automobiles passed.

The horses snorted and stamped their feet.

* * *

From the top of the rise down to the marshes, the highway was ablaze with the headlights of automobiles. The driverless wagon had slowed and held up traffic as far back as three quarters of a mile. Motorcycles and passenger cars filled the road.

The staccato wailing of patrol cars arriving filled the air over the milling crowd which had come to look. Patrol car after patrol car pushed its way through the excited gathering of people.

"I want the men in pairs," Colonel Schuckert was saying. "From Dachau down to the outskirts of Munich. In communication by radio. Sweep the marshes and the forests."

The sergeant saluted and moved to his subordinate, and the message was relayed down the line. Soon organization was being conducted at a rapid rate, with much loud talking by the patrol leaders. Two by two, with shotguns in their arms, or lanterns in their belts, they saluted Colonel Schuckert and moved into patrol cars, or began walking down the roads and into the fields.

"I am not in control of the case any longer," the Colonel said, turning to Steinman, "merely a traffic cop."

"Yes, sir," Steinman said.

A floodlight, bright blue-white and steaming through the fog, lit up the patrolmen nervously standing around the shoulder of the highway.

Steinman attempted to question the men and the woman from the wagon, who shuddered convulsively, as they sat on an overturned beer barrel at the shoulder of the road. But it was evident that the men had been oblivious to the world when it happened, and the woman was beyond self-control altogether. Steinman gestured to Koenig: "Cocoa, coffee, rum, anything to bring them out of it."

The fog burned past the floodlights, evaporating as it approached the white-hot carbon arcs and then closing in again from the other side. Sounds were obscurely muffled, as though they were being heard underwater, and a ghastly pall of unreality lay over the scene.

Dr. Karl-Heinz Fischer now climbed out of the embankment of the weeds. He carried a medical bag, and his shoes were stuck with long, muddy sticks. The crowd quieted momentarily as the doctor made his way through the cluster of uniformed policemen and ambulance drivers.

"Brandy, please," Dr. Fischer said. "Anything."

A patrol car pushed its way through the crowd. Protesting, the elements gave way. Dogs barked as the handsome man and woman inched through. They parked and Bauer stepped out.

"Paul," he said. "Why wasn't I told?"

Steinman looked darkly, hesitantly, at Bauer's face.

"Why wasn't my office informed?" Bauer demanded.

"Hugo Flanck's orders," Steinman said. "Sorry, Martin," he added.

Bauer's face darkened. He opened the door and Madeline stepped out of the car. The patrolmen behind Steinman saluted, but the Chief Inspector ignored them.

"Where is the body?" Bauer asked Fischer.

The doctor pointed to the embankment.

"Don't pull on anything," Fischer said, attempting a joke, "or it will come off."

Bauer led Madeline through the cluster of personnel to the edge of the road. There Colonel Schuckert looked up, somewhat startled to see them there.

"Oh, Bauer," Colonel Schuckert said. "I'm glad you came. It's been a bestial night." Pointing ahead, he said, "This way—"

The Colonel, moving his bulk clumsily up the embankment, slipped on a clump of mud. The wet came in and dirtied his knee. But Madeline and Bauer, ahead of him, did not notice. They stood on the top of the embankment, looking down into the beginning of the marsh.

"My God!" Bauer muttered.

Madeline put her hand to her mouth.

"He is quite strong, isn't he?" Colonel Schuckert said. "Come, come, Miss Kress. You must look at him now."

Madeline hesitated, but the Colonel took her arm and led her down the embankment, maneuvering as best he could through the weeds in front of them. Bauer, too, the nettles and burrs sticking to his socks and sleeves, moved wetly, suckingly, down through the mud.

Bauer knelt at the crumpled form in the mud. He wiped water from his brows. Dismay was written on his face.

Bauer looked at Madeline. "All right?" he asked gently.

"Go ahead," Madeline said.

Kneeling, Bauer felt the cold mud sinking through his pants leg. The Inspector reached down and carefully, gingerly, handled the dead man's head, turning it around and around until it faced them. The ease with which it turned sickened him.

"Do you know him?" Bauer asked.

"No," Madeline replied, bending still closer.

"He is just an old man," she said.

"But he must have been somebody once," Colonel Schuckert said. "A munitions driver, a cadet—"

"I don't know him from the records," she said. "Or personally."

Fog dripped from the weeds, making a quiet, steady sound. The single chime from St. Boniface tolled the quarter hour before midnight. A bird called—an owl—a long, hooting call, a mournful cry that echoed among the marsh trees and slowly died away.

"I fear," Colonel Schuckert said, "I fear he is killing Germans indiscriminately. He must have lost control altogether."

Bauer let the head sink down. It went several millimeters into the ground, a face which still had the marks of drunkenness softening the bruised portions of flesh. An old man who, with one eye, looked vacantly up into nothing.

"Well," Colonel Schuckert added, "I have orders to have him shot on sight."

Bauer laboriously retraced his steps through the mud, up the embankment, where the spectacle of the crowd greeted them. Like a painting from Ensor, the multicolored flesh in hues of red, pink, and yellow assembled under the brute arc lights; talking, joking, or merely waiting, curious, beyond the ropes, they had gathered in the hopes of seeing the dead man.

Steinman caught Bauer's eye at the edge of the crowd.

"They were my orders, Martin," Steinman protested.

"Where is he now?" Bauer asked.

"Flanck?"

"Flanck."

"Gone. He was here. He left. He went north with a car."

"North?"

"Yes."

"What's north? Another conference with the Minister?"

"Dachau," Colonel Schuckert said.

Bauer turned quickly. The Colonel was staring at the Gothic printing embossed in gilt on the side of the wagon. Bauer's eyes widened. The Colonel repeated to him.

"Dachau."

Bauer turned to Steinman.

"I want Berg and Modelle," he demanded. "Marksmen. Quickly!"

Steinman ran into the cluster of patrolmen.

A chorus of voices barked the names through the phalanx of police gathered there. Bauer saw the ambulance drivers stepping down off the embankment with the wicker full of a sagging form. Then two men, one in uniform, came rapidly toward him and the Colonel, saluting as they ran.

The Colonel, his bulk towering over them, listened as Bauer told them what he wanted. Then they went into their patrol cars and emerged carrying with them high-powered rifles. From a box inside the trunk of Bauer's car, they were given a small handful of bullets each, and they pointed their barrels toward the earth and slipped a bullet into the shiny black chambers, shielding it from the people and the veiling rain.

"I trust there will be no repercussions," the Colonel said, worried.

"Not to Dachau!" Madeline whispered to Bauer. "Please—I can't go there again!"

The Inspector turned. His eyes were wide. He, too, was afraid. "You must," he said simply. "You must!"

DACHAU:
The Sixteenth Day of Oktoberfest

CHAPTER NINETEEN

Arbeit Macht Frei, the faded letters read. Work Makes Free. The sign attached to the front gate of Dachau concentration camp was barely visible in the moonless night.

For twenty-eight years the concentration camp had been kept intact as a perpetual reminder of Hitler's ugly assault upon the human spirit. And though the setting today—the walls, the compound, and the buildings—suggested a benign, park-like atmosphere, the stark symbols of its notorious past still punctuated the serene vista like the choked cries of its countless dead.

Sharp pikes decorated the top of the thick walls. A black gate hung between heavy stone pillars, the grillework of wrought iron guarding the road from the terrible contents within.

Arbeit Macht Frei.

Long, low buildings loomed out of the shadows of the compound. They were made of wood, pale now, where a fleeting light from the road caught them. Shadows of the trees danced over their walls. There was no other movement. There was no sound.

Arbeit Macht Frei.

Outside the gate, Flanck loaded the bullets into the chambers of his snub-nosed revolver. Behind him were Patrolmen Kirst and Modersohn. Kirst wore rimless spectacles, and both carried rifles in their gloved hands.

Flanck looked into the courtyard. Well-kept lawns disappeared between the buildings. Flowers and wreaths gave a pale color to the night. Dirt paths led to larger brick buildings. Flanck leaned against the gate, peering into the dark areas of the compound.

The paths were deserted. Slabs of stone with inscriptions, electric wires leading to metal boxes threw crisscrosses of shadows over the dirt. Barbed wire rose, tangled, under the machine-gun towers.

Flanck pushed lightly upon the black iron gate. It gave way slowly. A steel chain, which had fastened the two huge doors, was broken, twisted off with incredible strength by an iron bar, and now both bar and chain fell to the ground. They clanged, and the noise echoed throughout the compound.

Flanck knew this was the final moment. Fear curled around his brain. It shivered up his spine and made his hands cold. His face was pale. Nervously, he turned to the patrolmen behind him and said, "Let us conclude the matter."

The doors swung open, and there in the central courtyard, unobstructed to their view, was a small bronze statue of a Jew, emaciated and dying, leaning subtly forward, the metal face pock-marked and edged in shadow.

Flanck and the patrolmen entered the Dachau compound.

A look of distaste contorted Flanck's face.

"One day soon, we will burn these places down. Wipe them off the face of German soil."

The patrolmen nodded in nervous agreement.

*   *   *

Speeding up the highway, a patrol car swerved uncertainly through the villages north of Munich, through the stone streets, surrounded by the Bavarian homes, the rose gardens and white fences, then out into the dark countryside once more.

"Faster, Koenig," Bauer said.

Koenig's eyes widened. He looked up quickly from the steering wheel, into the Chief Inspector's face, and swallowed. Already the patrol car was going faster than he could possibly have braked against.

Barn walls, dilapidated wagons, and embankments of weeds flew past Koenig's vision. The headlights swept around the curves of the country road. A cat screamed for safety and leaped out of the way. Insects, blinded, were caught in the brightness of the headlights, and then flew back into darkness again.

Bauer, Schuckert, and Madeline looked impassively ahead.

Colonel Schuckert put a finger under the stiff collar of his uniform, as though he were deprived of air. The granite face was grim and immobile, but the eyes were bloodshot, steeled against the oncoming, rushing night.

"Shall this all be over soon?" Colonel Schuckert said.

"I pray so, sir," Bauer answered.

Bauer opened the window a bit in the front seat. The wind whipped up the thinning dark hair, making it unruly. For an instant, Bauer looked like a very tired, depleted man.

"I very much pray so, sir," Bauer said.

Madeline pushed herself back into the upholstery of the rear seat, as though she could counteract the motion of the car which hurtled her, deliriously, at one hundred kilometers per hour toward the compound outside of Dachau village.

*   *   *

A flashlight played over the long wooden shingles of the barracks. The glass in the windows reflected the beam as a pale glimmer. The panes were dirty. In the interior of the buildings there was total darkness. Only the vague shapes of crude beds loomed out of the blackness. The flashlight could not penetrate. On the walls, the shadows of trees danced and swayed, and swooped down, suddenly, in quick gusts of wind.

"He is here!" Flanck whispered between his teeth. "I know he is here!"

Flanck walked down the central road of Dachau compound. Behind him, rifles at chest height, walked the two men in uniform. Flanck's black shiny shoes kicked up the dirt. Bits of dust rose and fell at every step, and only slowly drifted back onto the road. Shadows that they created undulated wildly with every step they took.

"You have no other light?" Flanck whispered.

The patrolmen shook their heads, almost imperceptibly.

"Stupid!" Flanck said. "Very stupid, indeed!"

The wind shook suddenly through the large trees behind the observation towers. It threw dead, yellowed leaves into the air. Insects chirped. The wind, dying, let bits of twigs, dead matter, fall down onto the roofs of the barracks, over the fences and walls of the concentration camp.

"Go to the north corner," Flanck said. "Stay together. Come toward me at a diagonal. Try to find the light switch. There must be one here. I know there is."

The patrolmen nodded and hurriedly left Flanck.

Flanck stood isolated. He stood now between two rows of prisoners' barracks. The small glass windows looked blank, like

eyes. The Administration Building was somewhere ahead, beyond the bronze Jew and past the stone slabs with wreaths.
Flanck headed slowly down the long, thin path between the
barracks. He held the flashlight in the left hand and the short
revolver in the right.

The barracks, as he passed, seemed not to know the inter-
vening years. They were well kept. The surfaces were newly
painted. The steps were restored. Only a little dust danced in
his light beam as he passed. He walked over dark green lawns
which ended abruptly at each row of barracks.

*   *   *

Inside each barracks building were long rows of bunks. In
each crude bunk bed, a sheet had been placed, and under the
sheet was straw, giving the eerie impression of human form.

The long wooden floors were swept clean. Wooden shelves
were neatly but crudely affixed to the walls. But for the twigs
falling upon the roofs, and rolling down, or the breezes that
subtly shook the glass in the panes, there was no sound. There
was no movement.

"Ilse?"

In the darkness of the room, the floors creaked of their own
accord. The sheets were faintly visible under the windows. Outside, a passing light, held in Flanck's hand, bobbed quickly
through the window, throwing shadows of the rectangular
cross panes down the length of the barracks wall, and then
disappeared.

"Ilse?" Hass's voice whispered urgently.

But no one was alive. No one heard.

Hass's labored breathing came from beneath a bunk. His hand
reached up to the sheets and pulled them aside. It felt straw.
Long, yellowish sticks of straw pricked the hard flesh.

Hass's mind rebelled. He tried to see, tried to clarify the
form of a face in that hallucination. Hass peered down sideways,

trying to penetrate the darkness, and whispered to the straw form.

"She is a Polish Jew. She has a Polish accent, speaks German. She is blond, thin, and very beautiful."

Hass leaned forward, closer, and put his ear down into the straw.

"She speaks German," he said. "And a child. Anna. Age seven. Have you seen her? Please, God, do you know where she is?"

But whomever he talked to must be dead. In the silence, Hass understood something terrible. He went down the aisle, disturbing the straw forms under the sheets.

"Is anyone alive here?" Hass whispered, pleading.

He leaned against the wall, perspiring. The huge, heavy head was weak with lack of sleep. It was grimy, lined in creases of exhaustion. He breathed heavily.

"Not even one?" he murmured.

Suddenly there were voices from the outside. Hass turned quickly and, pressing himself back against the wall, looked out into the compound behind the barracks.

Through the window in the crisscross of cold blue lights, he saw men digging with shovels. They wore filthy striped uniforms. Their eyes were sunken. Their jaws were slack. The limbs were narrow, far narrower than the joints which seemed to bulge out from the emaciated flesh.

Some of the men could not stand, but leaned, as though waiting, on the shoulders of those who could still work.

Around them were the German guards. The guards were not well dressed, but wore dingy, rumpled fatigues, and they were unshaven. There was a peculiar dead quality to their faces, as if dead weights had replaced their minds, and they stood as though half dead themselves.

The *Rapportführer* put down his clip board.

"Who among you is a twin?" the *Rapportführer* asked.

The prisoners only looked back with animal eyes.

"Come, come," the *Rapportführer* said. "I need three more sets."

Not a man moved or stirred to open his mouth.

"I assure you, it is quite painless. You will be taken care of. Two hot meals a day and stationery privileges."

The *Rapportführer* moved down the row. He stopped at the cart into which the dirt was being piled. In front of him was a small man whose eyesight was ruined, for he stared up with a terrible squint.

"Go to the Infirmary," the *Rapportführer* said.

The small man, his pajamas flapping loosely about his skinny legs, looked up stupidly at the *Rapportführer*.

The *Rapportführer*, suddenly, without warning, struck the man in the face with a gloved fist. The man crumpled to the ground. The *Rapportführer* moved down the row.

He stopped in front of a man with a narrow chest, coughing soundlessly, leaning on his shovel.

"Take him to the Infirmary," the *Rapportführer* said.

Without a word, the man with the narrow chest bent low and hurriedly picked up the legs of the small man with the poor eyesight. The *Rapportführer* watched with satisfaction. He drew a line on his clip board.

"This is terrible!" he said. "You are dying too slowly!"

He turned back to face the assembled prisoners. Behind him, throwing a weird red light upon his flesh, was the dark glow at the top of the tall brick chimneys. The colors undulated upon his cheeks and made his eyes go dark.

"Don't you understand?" the *Rapportführer* said. "We haven't much time! The war will be over soon!"

Just then, a train rumble filled the night air. It was a faraway sound, coming out of Munich, and the whistle reverberated, long, lonely, and sad. The ground shook, and the sound passed away. The *Rapportführer*'s face, livid in the distant, reddish glow, twitched in fear.

Hass pressed himself further against the wall. He trembled. Final selection was being conducted. They no longer selected, but threw everyone indiscriminately—

A flashlight came in through the window, pouring over the sheeted bunks. Hass crept down. The lone, pale light source flashed through the dirty window panes, iridescent. It passed over Hass's head and was cut off by the edge of the window.

Hass counted to ten, then cautiously opened the door. The *Rapportführer* and the guards had taken the prisoners away as rapidly and mysteriously as they had come. The compound was silent, deserted. Hass saw no one. The German with the flashlight had disappeared around the far corner.

Hass looked around. He left the barracks and quickly ran up the walk to the next building. With horror, he realized that the door was hooked from the inside.

Hass, trembling and perspiring, jerked and heaved at the door. "Let me in!" he whispered. "I'm a Jew!"

In the far courtyard, the marksman with the rimless spectacles put his hand upon the arm of the other patrolman.

"What was that?"

"What?" the other whispered.

"I'm not sure. Maybe I heard something."

The patrolman with the rimless glasses pushed the other from him, so that they were more spread out and thus, several meters apart, they converged slowly on the south end of the barracks.

In the darkness, Hass had found a way in.

He had dropped down under a forced window. Now he found himself in a dark, square room. He felt his way down a corridor. There were black hooks in long rows on the wall. By using them, Hass felt his way down through the narrow passage and came to a small chamber.

There was no door, no windows, and but one outlet—the corridor down which he had come.

The ceiling was high. The walls were rough and plastered. A

huge iron door, half a meter thick, was swung open in front of him.

"Ilse?"

Hass peered in through the doorway.

Short metal shower heads appeared in rows over his head. They were dark, silhouetted from behind, as the far wall reflected a wan light. The metal fixtures looked like little animal heads. Peculiar. Sturdy. Alive. They seemed to wink at Hass.

"Ilse?"

Hass had the terrible premonition that they were going to speak to him. They glittered in the wan reflective light, and scintillated at him in the chamber.

—There's a secret here, Hass heard them whisper. —Do you know what it is? —Just a little secret!—

Trembling shook him from his bones and into his brains. For an instant, a black hole threatened to come up from nowhere for him, but then he regained consciousness. Hass threw his hands up against the shower heads, desperately, but the sounds of his exertion—shuffling and heavy breathing in the shower chamber—echoed and died slowly around him.

—There's no water in these pipes. Not the slightest bit of water in *these* pipes!—

The metal fixtures winked at him.

—Do you want to find your wife? Well, she is not here now. She was here, but she is not here, now—

"No! No!" Hass gasped.

Hass covered his face with his hands, as though to press away sight itself from his eyeballs. He stumbled from the shower chamber, through the iron-rimmed doorway, and stumbled down the corridors. Hass bumped and stumbled against the wall, and thudded heavily against the doorjamb of a larger, colder chamber.

"Am I mad?" Hass thought, catching his breath. He held onto the edge of the chamber door. "Adonai, oh, please, no more of this!"

Hugo Flanck, in the far corner of the courtyard, threw down a short, electrical switch.

"Just so!" Flanck exclaimed.

Brightness flashed upon Hass, whiter than the day. He shielded his eyes, but there, in front of his outspread fingers, were the ovens. Large, metal rimmed, with valves and steel handles on the doors, they gaped open in a row. They opened their mouths, nestled in a huge brick wall. Conveyor belts from the shower chamber glittered and glistened in the brilliant light.

Hass screamed, then crumpled to the floor.

Flanck's ears pricked up.

"Did you hear that?" he whispered.

In the south end of the barracks, the patrolmen waved back that they had heard. Flanck signaled them to move around the crematorium walls in a surrounding maneuver. He then raced down the long row between the prisoners' barracks. His feet flew over the pleasant grass lawn. Flanck held his revolver out in front of him, and studied the chamber walls. He walked up to the forced window.

He shone the flashlight down into the corridor of clothes hooks.

"He is most assuredly in there!" Flanck said.

Flanck climbed up, awkwardly, into the window, and then dropped down inside. He walked noiselessly down the corridor.

Flanck paused. At the end of a waiting chamber, the small screen door had swung shut. He could not see inside. Flanck lightly pushed the door open.

In front of him, on the stone floor, a huge man in dirty blue rags bowed and bent, moaning in unutterable agony.

"What—" Flanck muttered, in disbelief. "Praying—?"

For an instant, Flanck was a dark form, lit from behind, in the narrow doorway.

Then, with a lunge so sudden it caught Flanck by surprise, Hass leaped ahead and crashed into him. Flanck's head smashed violently against the doorjamb. The door gave way, splintering. Flanck felt the hands close around his throat, squeezing with a strength he could not believe. Flanck saw brightness, felt himself breaking inside. His fingers pulled on the trigger again and again. The explosions roared in the huge chambers.

Hass's right leg buckled, broken and bleeding.

Flanck twisted away, holding his throat. His revolver, useless, scuttled along the ground. He wheeled, flailed at the corridors, choking, sucking for air, but no air came to him. He stumbled down into the darkness and tried to support himself by the shower heads, but the heads, not true water fixtures, snapped off in his hands, and he fell heavily to the stone floor. Dust and plaster followed him down, rose about him, and obscured the chamber.

"I can't breathe!" Flanck tried to yell, but only a high-pitched scream emerged.

Flanck struggled toward the door, but as he reached it, Hass's huge fist lashed out and struck him under the jaw. The shock smashed his jaw. Flanck felt blood seeping up through parts of his face. He fell down through the doorway into the night air, and tumbled down a short flight of stairs.

"Kirst! Modersohn!" Flanck yelled in a gasp of air.

God in Heaven! Flanck thought. I am going to die!

Down the steps, after him, powerfully, crab-like, came the huge Jew, dragging his useless leg after him.

Flanck pulled himself backward, dimly seeing. Each time he moved, needles of pain shot into his head.

Hass was upon him, crawling for the legs, the shoes, the body of Flanck. Flanck pitched forward into darkness, arms flailing uselessly upon the ground.

"Hass!" boomed a voice of authority.

Hass heard nothing and pulled Flanck by the head to a rock on the ground. There he lifted Flanck's head high over the stone and prepared to smash it down.

"Hass! Let him live!"

Hass looked up. They had surrounded him. Germans stood at the gates of the compound with their revolvers drawn. Spotlights, headlights of patrol cars, flooded his eyes.

"Watch me!" Hass answered. His teeth gritted, he wept in hatred, and lifted Flanck's head higher over the stone.

"*Hass!!*" screamed a woman's voice.

Hass's head jerked as though it had been shot.

Bauer, breathing hard, and Schuckert and Madeline had raced into the compound. The headlights of the patrol cars silhouetted them, made radiances around their shadowy forms.

Madeline came forward.

"*Hass!*" she cried.

Her face was lost in shadow but her hair streamed behind her, translucent. Only her gray eyes, brilliant and luminescent, seemed to shine in that woman's face. It was a face that looked down on Hass from another world.

Hass, trembling, stared, shocked, confused. He was hypnotized, transfixed.

"Willi," Madeline said in Yiddish. "What have they done to you?"

Again, Hass's head jerked at the sound of his name.

Who was she? Was she an earthly being at all? And why didn't they shoot? What were they waiting for? With fascination, Hass watched her advance. Did she have nothing in her hands? The women were always the worst.

"Oh, Willi, Willi." Madeline wept.

Hass tried to focus his eyes. But all he saw was the form of the woman, outlined in the brilliant lights around them. Something wet and bright in the eyes— She was coming closer, ever closer, her face strange, taut, thin, and her long hair bright and unkempt around her neck. Ilse?

Hass's face shivered in unutterable joy and an agony of disbelief. He leaned forward, letting Flanck's head fall from his grip.

"Ilse?"

Bauer stepped quickly from the shadows of the trees.

"Make him come to you!" he whispered hoarsely.

Madeline stood, isolated at the center of the brilliant compound, transfixed, over the spectacle of the Jew, crippled, deranged, who crawled toward her at her feet.

Hass pulled himself up by her skirt. He knelt before her and peered upward fearfully.

"Ilse?"

Tears streamed down Madeline's face. She brushed the hair from her eyes. Hass's heavy head looked up at her from her waist. She touched the huge face with her slender fingers.

"It's all right, now," she murmured brokenly.

Madeline knelt. She put her arms around Hass and he burst into tears; he clutched her madly to himself.

"Who am I if not Ilse?" Madeline whispered.

She cradled the weeping face against her shoulder, and the tears streamed rapidly from both their faces.

"It's all right, now, Willi," she repeated.

Around the compound, unmoving, were the host of German policemen. Young, for the most part, they stared with taut faces at the two Jews embracing in the courtyard.

Bauer stood over them, casting his shadow upon them. Madeline looked up, her face tear-tracked, helpless, then looked down again, and held Hass's head against hers.

"It's all right, now, Willi." She wept.

Bauer reached down a hand to help them up, but was afraid, and refrained. As in Paris, as in Yad Vashem, a dry fire seemed to eat at his bones, and he felt dizzy and sick with shame. He raised a hand. Koenig slowly came from the group of watching patrolmen.

"Turn down the lights," Bauer whispered to him.

Another patrolman came forward, a sergeant, and brought bandages with him. Madeline pulled up the pants leg, and soothed Hass, who continued to cling to her as though he could not get close enough.

Past the pedestal of the central bronze memorial, Flanck was carefully being lifted onto a stretcher. His eyes were dark with the sight of death, and his clothes torn, his hair disheveled. Gradually the two attendants placed the stretcher into a waiting ambulance which immediately raced out onto the open highway toward Munich.

Colonel Schuckert, standing under the trees where the insects had gathered, watched, motionless, from a protective shadow.

"Why doesn't Koenig hurry?" Bauer said aloud, looking out into the brightly lit compound.

Finally the lights began to dim, first one, then the other, changing color a little, so that the shadows grew and fell and the highlights of the bronze statue seemed to leap and fall, like flames, as the cross beams died alternately. Soon it was dark again, and Bauer stood under the imposing statue.

"Come, Koenig," Bauer said, as Koenig rapidly came from the interior. "We are finished here."

Madeline and the sergeant eased the moaning, babbling Hass into the back seat of Bauer's personal patrol car, and Madeline and Bauer sat on either side of the sobbing Jew.

In the front seat, Colonel Schuckert sat down heavily, blinking his eyes rapidly.

Bauer leaned back uncomfortably. Koenig got behind the wheel and started the engine.

At the gate, Bauer instructed a single patrolman to guard the gate until the morning.

"Make sure no children enter," he added. "You know what to do."

"Exactly, sir."

The patrolman saluted.

Madeline continued to hold Hass, as the car drove off rapidly toward Munich.

The villages raced by, tucked against the darker hills. The clouds had formed into long silver fingers. Cows slept in the half-opened doors of stone farms. It was the quintessence of German isolation, of a cold autumn night, and the Bavarian homes with their little alleys, the rose boxes at the upper windows, flew by, and seemed forever mysterious, fascinating. But now, for Bauer, the heart of it was forever eaten away, and a terrible void and loneliness had come to take its place.

Bauer rubbed his eyes.

With horror, he realized that Hass had taken hold of his hand. Bauer turned and met Hass's dark, deep, tear-filled eyes, which directed themselves straight into Bauer's brain.

Bauer swallowed.

He tried to speak but could not.

He gradually withdrew his hand. Hass leaned once more, moaning softly, on Madeline's shoulder. Bauer covered his hand where Hass had touched it.

"Who shall take care of him now?" Bauer asked, after a long stillness.

"We shall," answered Madeline's exhausted voice from the other side of the seat.

Bauer looked out of the window at the impenetrable blackness of the empty countryside.

"Well," he said quietly. "We shall see. We shall have to see about that." And then, with a sigh of weariness, he added, "Thank God, it's over."

"Is it?" Madeline said softly. "Will it ever be over?"

Far behind them, in the Dachau compound, all was dark. The emaciated Jew stood forlorn. At his feet were inscriptions, unreadable in the dark. At his side were wreaths of old flowers. He was a silhouette, a shadow made of bronze, in the form of a dying man, high on a stone block. There was no one to watch over him, no one to care for him, save the lone patrolman who sat on the bench guarding the broken gate until dawn, and he much preferred to keep his eye upon the lovely form of the sleepy little village of Dachau.